SPHERES

V. ANGELO

To Mom, Dad, and Mi Hermano.
Thank you for always supporting me.

To my husband. You're my favorite.

cry (krī)

verb

A state of sadness – *never cry when you are melancholy*

sorrow

A state of frustration or anger – *never cry when you are mad*

heartache

A state of grief – *never cry when you are mourning*

devastation

A state of shedding tears – *never cry from your eyes*

unhappiness

V. ANGELO

Despite the warm breeze, my headphones are chilly against my neck. Clenching my boom pole in front of me to keep my sweaty palms from losing grip, the hairs on the top of my hands stand as if they are soldiers awaiting commands. Standing frozen, my eyes slowly shift to take in the chaos around me.

Black figures climb over each other to secure exploding white umbrellas. Fast moving mouths are screaming as hardened hands furiously scribble on clipboards. Bright long fingernails delicately punch powder onto a soft, already rosy cheek. Careful arms tightly screw minuscule locks into even more minuscule pockets.

"The magic hour doesn't last forever people!"

Shattering my gaze, I revert my focus to an older man speeding across the chaos, the black pom pom from his hat bouncing up and down. He stops in the middle of it all, circling around to see everyone.

"How long does it take to plug in a few wires and adjust a light or two! It's," he looks down at his watch, squinting, "five forty two, we only have seventeen more minutes. Let's wrap this up people," he shouts making his way towards the camera crew, pom pom still bouncing. I let go of the boom with my hand, leaving behind a watery outline of my palm. I quickly use my shirtsleeve to remove my sweat.

"What did you do this time," a familiar voice behind me asks.

"You know," I reply, inspecting the boom pole. "I heard booms these days are made with secret compartments in them."

"Really?"

"Yup," I nod.

"Can I take part in this buried treasure?"

"Nope."

"Oh come on Rose, spread the wealth!"

"Finders keepers," I smirk. "What are you doing here, I thought you were not on call today?"

"I wasn't, but they needed a *tall* crew member for the reflectors today."

"Ah yes, Chard to the rescue!"

"As always," he smiles. I do not know how he does it, but his teeth are always white. One could be in a dark room and instead of asking for a candle, Chard flashing his smile would work just fine. Chard and I became friends a few months back. His real name is Charden but most people call him Chard. He works the lighting on set and I work the sound. Usually crew members do not interact with crew members outside their Department, but Chard and I are a rare exception I guess.

"I see they got you on boom again," Chard says, pointing slyly to the cylinder secured in my hands.

"Yup. Not surprised though, it has become a reoccurring theme."

"Then you must be an expert by this point," he replies, flashing his smile again.

"Time is of the essence people, sixteen more minutes. We need the reflectors in place and camera on the slider," pom pom man frantically states to the crew.

"Why is he so angry, we still got sixteen minutes left," I ask.

"Come on Rose," Chard says, running his hands through his stubbly brown hair. "You should know by now the director is always the craziest one."

"Yeah," rolling my eyes. "They should have hired back the director from last month, he was incredible."

"You didn't hear?" Chard asks puzzled. I shake my head in confusion. Chard exhales slowly. "He lost all his spheres, he's at Amella now." I can feel the blood draining from my face, the grip on my boom loosening. "Something about his wife cheating on him. Had a breakdown, guess he couldn't handle it. He had four left too. I feel bad for the guy," Chard says softly.

Lost all of them? At Amella now?

"But hey," Chard smirks, elbowing my now stiffened arm. "We still got all six of ours, right?"

"Yup," I fake a smile and nod. "Still going strong."

"One minute until filming, take your marks," a production manager yells.

"Well guess I better head back," Chard says. "Good to see you Rose." He leaves with a wink, jogging back to his mark.

'He lost all his spheres, he's at Amella now.'

Chard's words pulsate through my mind repeatedly. How could that be? He had four last month. *Four.* How did he lose them all so quickly? I faintly hear the director requesting the actress as my bones tighten and my gaze becomes hazy. I re-play Chard's response in my head. *'He lost all his spheres, he's at Amella now.'*

The warm breeze stings across the top of my hands. The headphones around my neck suffocate me. Deeper and deeper my nails dig into my tender skin. My body is numb, but my eyes stop this feeling. It is a feeling I have had before, but I will never show. The feeling of crying. To let tears fall down your cheek. To let your eyes display pain, misery, empathy. Though I can never do it. Not in this world.

I blink away my thoughts, immersing myself into the rushing wildness once again. I release my tight grip on the boom and remove my choking headphones from my neck, allowing me to breathe a little easier. On autopilot, I hit my mark, and as I plant my feet in place, I brace myself for lights, camera, action.

Trying to push the news Chard gave me in the back of my mind, I focus on what I am here to do. I remain on my mark, awaiting the actress' arrival. Director pom pom blows through the set, claiming his chair behind the camera.

"Where's the talent!" he yells over his shoulder.

Standing out among the sea of black, our talent is radiant upon her entrance. Her auburn, pixie hair shines as it swallows the lighting. Round, baby blue eyes hypnotize all, as soft red butterfly lips separate to display a wall of white teeth. Revealing every curve, a royal blue pencil dress clings to her body while a dip in the front allows cleavage to peek out ever so subtly. She is captivating. She is doing her job.

As she carefully walks to her mark, hair and makeup crew continue to pamper her. Perfection is of the utmost importance. No flaws. No mishaps. The real captivator though is under her eyes, displaying six tiny white circles. Three under her right eye, three under her left eye. Hair and makeup drift away as she takes her stance in front of the camera.

Anticipation weighs on everyone as we await the final seconds. I secure my headphones and raise my arms up, the boom hovering over the actress. A manager announces for everyone to be quiet on the set. The director shoots his hand up, spreading all his fingers counting down for everyone to see and hear.

"Five, four, three, two," mouthing the word one. The red light glows on the camera. The actress begins reciting her lines.

"Hello, Northerners. Amella would like to wish a Happy Counting to you all.

Tomorrow marks our thirty sixth hundredth Counting here in the States and my how far we have come. Three hundred years ago humans were weak, frail, and delicate. Weeping in public, mourning the death of others, crying from injury. But thanks to Amella there are no more tears and no more crying. The States can now produce strong, powerful, and forceful humans with the help of spheres. Spheres allow us to limit our cries so we, the Northerners, can be seen as the strongest. The less tears we shed, the more powerful we become." The actress flashes a smile, taking a pause before continuing her lines.

"Each of us have six horizontal spheres which we acquire at birth. Three under our right eye, three under our left eye. Each of us are trained during infancy to extinct the action of crying. Influences from outside sources have been eliminated to keep this extinction of emotion. No music, no books, no entertainment that can trigger negative emotions. Only positivity. But in the event that one does shed a tear, one will lose a sphere. And remember, the less spheres you have, the less quality life you can experience in the States." The actress flashes her smile again.

"Counting Five of this year will begin tomorrow at eleven o'clock outside North Amella. If you need to refill your spheres, do so by curfew tonight in order for the North to keep its slot as number one. Keep your spheres and do not shed your tears. Happy Counting Northerners." The actress remains smiling, staring into the camera's lens.

"Cut!"

The red light fades from the camera and the tranquility is broken with chaos once again. My arms collapse and I quickly release my ears from their headphones.

"Good job people," pom pom director says. "Let's clean and start editing so we can get this video out today before curfew."

Crew members start milling about and disassembling the set. I walk over to the sound station, setting down my equipment in its appropriate place. Mimicking teeth on a comb, I use my fingers to brush my hair. As I am fixing my hair, the actress is back with hair and makeup. She is sitting in a chair, mannequin like, while the crew deconstruct her. While hands wiggle underneath her wig to reveal her true buzzed, blonde hair another crew member uncovers her face. The actress looks to the sky as her blue contacts are extracted, leaving behind her canyon brown eyes. Her radiance begins to slowly diminish. Starting with the right eye, a crew member peals away one sphere, then another, then another, and one more. The crew member stops and the actress stands to change, disappearing behind a curtain.

Two spheres? This glowing actress who just happily smiled in front of an entire audience only has two spheres? With the makeup and outfit gone, she looks as if she is normal. Funny how true features are revealed once the fake are erased.

The actress approaches me as she walks off the set, and I realize that I have been staring at her for quite some time. Before I can pretend to look like I am busy, our eyes meet. Closer now, I can see her upper cheeks are sprinkled with freckles. She seemed so happy in front of the camera, but her eyes tell a different story. I finally grab my belongings, slumping my backpack over my shoulder. My eyes search for Chard. They meet and I give him a quick wave, him giving me a two finger salute in return. I turn on my heels and begin my walk home.

***

I stare down at my sneakers, listening to them crunch on top of pebbles. My ears pick up the sound of the pebbles echoing and I look up to see the actress a little ahead of me. I begin to walk faster to catch up to her but I stop.

What am I doing?

She has two spheres, but it is not my place to ask why that is, I do not even know her name. I decide to travel a different way home and let her be. She is a two after all. A walk alone can comfort a sorrowful mind. I take one last look at her, the *real* her. Not the actress standing in front of the camera, but the plain girl walking home. Then my feet do the moving and I let her go on her way and me on mine.

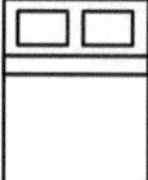

I silently close the front door behind me as I enter my house. Noiseless. Being as soft as possible, I quietly make my way towards the kitchen. Without warning, I topple over a pile of shoes, breaking the silence. I stop, closing my eyes to listen. Nothing. I exhale in relief; I did not wake anyone.

Not wanting to risk it again, I scoot around the shoes to my bedroom. I decide to head back to sleep because no one is up, not my parents, not my neighbors, not even anyone in the North. Soundlessly shutting the door behind me, I crumble into bed, letting tiredness command my eyes shut.

***

Opening my eyes, I take a big breath in through my nose, and stretch my entire body. Exhaustion begins to creep back into my mind, but the phone interrupts that feeling. I fumble to find the source of the vibration on my nightstand. Without even looking at the number, I groggily answer the phone.

"Hello?" I faintly ask.

"Are you sleeping?"

"Yes," I yawn and rub my eyes. "Why are you calling at this hour?"

"Rose, it's almost noon," the other line states bluntly. I turn my head to see my clock on the table which reads 11:43.

"You are over exaggerating," I state, still disoriented. "It is almost eleven forty five."

"Sue me for rounding up. We can pick up Stevey and then get lunch, or for you breakfast." I nod in agreement. "I'm gonna assume you're nodding." I nod again. "I'll see you at the school." The call is ended and I secure the phone in its holder.

Bringing my hand to my face, I drag my fingertips under my eye. Smooth then rough, smooth then rough, smooth then rough. Feeling the disconnect between my skin and my spheres. Six spheres. I have always been labeled a six. I finally stagger out of bed, starting the day again for me. For Rose. A six.

***

There are already mothers fencing in the school before dismissal as they wait for their child. Amid this pile of dapper mothers, there she is. Jejune. My best friend, sticking out like a sore thumb, just as the actress this morning stood out amongst our crew members. Unlike the actress, Jejune does not attract attention due to captivating beauty but rather… eccentricity.

Per usual, you can always find Jejune in a hat. It is her trademark. Although she is facing away from me, her features and trademark hat do not give me clues in identifying her. The mothers are standing a good distance away from her. Jejune works in the Food Industry, specifically the Fishing Department. Being around her for so long, I have become immune to her stench.

"You sure do have a habit of driving people away," I state, taking my place next to her.

"Nah, they're just jealous," she smirks. Today she is wearing a brown baseball cap with the letters "JJ" stitched in the middle, short for Jejune. Three arching white circles on the top and three arching white circles on the bottom surround her initials. The design on her hat is the same design logo for Amella but JJ is encircled as opposed to Amella. This is Jejune's subtle middle finger to Amella. "Glad to see you're awake," she continues.

"Hey," I snap back. "I had an early shift, we had to film at the magic hour," I say, providing air quotes.

"So did I," Jejune snaps back. "Well, not the magic hour part, but the early shift part."

"I can see that," I state looking her up and down. Her boots are laced with crusted mud and dried grime is peeling from her saucy gold skin. The only pop of color are the blue and purple bruises surrounding her knees. "You could have taken a shower at least."

"Well some people have other jobs after their jobs, like picking up their loved ones from school," she groans, glaring at the mothers.

The mothers could have been staring at Jejune due to her smell. If I had to guess though, that is not the reason why the mothers were glancing in Jejune's direction. Along with the silent whispers, I could detect the mothers were staring at Jejune's face, specifically under her eye, the right eye. Where her outermost sphere should be is instead a deep, crimson scar. Her scar resembles a disfigured circle with short, wavy lines shooting out in all directions.

Jejune has never told me how that scar got there, but because of her scar, Jejune can have at most five spheres. Instead of having the luxury of being a six, she is a five which is not too bad. It is better than being a two or one or worse, a zero. But people like these mothers outside of the school, who stare and whisper, demonstrate although it is just a small blemish, her scar speaks volumes. As Jejune looks to her far left to see the mothers, the bloodshot corner of her eye can be seen. Another permanent injury from her scar.

"Bitches," she mumbles under her breath.

The staring match is interrupted as children exit the building. Jejune looks back front towards the school, the bloodshot in her eye vanishing. Jejune wobbles on her tippy toes searching for her little brother. She crouches down to his level and he barrels into her, almost knocking off his glasses in the process.

"Whoa there buddy!" Jejune yells, catching him at the last second. He begins laughing, stepping back from Jejune and sloppily straightening out his glasses.

"JJ you stink!" he states in his innocent voice.

"Really?" she questions. Jejune lifts up her arm and takes in a big sniff. "I think I smell goooood," she elongates, rubbing her armpit in Stevey's face.

"Ew JJ stop!" he squeals in between giggles.

"Look who came to join us for lunch today," Jejune says, gesturing to where I am standing. Stevey squints as he looks up, his round face taking in the blaring sun. He gives a little smirk and timidly waves.

"Hey Rose."

"Hi Stevey," I reply back with a smile.

"I see you've met my star student," a soft voice says in front of us.

"What this little guy," Jejune asks, tickling Stevey's shoulders. "Nah you're just saying that because Rose is here," Jejune jokingly states.

"I can assure you it is not because of that," the woman laughs. The woman I am referring to is Stevey's reading teacher who is also my mother. My mom and I have been told we could be sisters we look so much alike. Slim figure, short brown hair, oval shaped brown eyes. We even have the same bunny nose and butterfly pink lips. It is as if I am looking in a mirror but with one less sphere under my eye.

"So where are you girls off to," my mom asks.

"Gonna grab some lunch with this one," Jejune says, rubbing Stevey's blonde hair so hard he has to hold onto his glasses.

"It's going to be delicious," Stevey announces.

"That's a big word," Jejune proclaims, raising her eyebrows in surprise.

"Mrs. Elle taught it to us in school today," Stevey beams.

"Yes I did," my mom says smiling, kneeling down to meet his eye level. "But I have a question for you Stevey." He bites his lower lip, happily awaiting her question. "Do you remember how to spell delicious?" Panicked, he quickly looks up at Jejune for reassurance.

"Go on," she tells him.

"Delicious," Stevey repeats and closes his eyes. "D.E.L.I.C—I.O.U.S." he finishes, opening his eyes.

"Very good Stevey," my mom smiles, standing back up. "Well you guys have fun, and don't be out too late, tomorrow is a big day," the last part being directed towards me.

"Don't worry I'll have her home by curfew," Jejune winks.

"I will see you tonight," I say to my mom. She exhales, wrapping her arms around me.

"I'll be worried. You know it's Counting Day tomorrow."

"I know mom," I reply, releasing from our embrace. She timidly nods and makes her way back to the school.

"So little man what do you want for lunch?" Jejune asks as we begin to leave, Stevey grabbing her hand.

"I dunno," he says, shrugging his shoulders.

"Rose?" Jejune asks, her and Stevey swinging their arms back and forth.

"I am good with anything."

"Well aren't you two just so helpful," Jejune replies. "The usual it is."

Surprisingly when we arrive, the shop is not lively. Just a few construction workers on their lunch breaks. We make our route to the weighing station. Each of us step onto a scale, clicking on our appropriate age and gender. The scale beeps as my number appears: 119.3 lbs. I, along with Jejune and Stevey, step off our scales and head to the counter.

"What can I get for you," a heavyset man asks. I motion for Jejune and Stevey to go ahead first.

"I'll have a tomato salad and this one here will have a peanut butter and jelly sandwich," Jejune says.

"And a sugar cookie!" Stevey yells, pointing to the individually wrapped cookies on the counter.

"And a sugar cookie," Jejune adds.

"I'm sorry ma'am he cannot have the sugar cookie," the man states.

"Excuse me?" Jejune asks in confusion.

"I can't allow it," he simply states. "But the boy can still have the sandwich."

"What do you mean you *can't* allow it," Jejune snaps back.

"According to the scale, this boy is fifty two point seven pounds and he should be at fifty one pounds for his age, he is overweight."

"*Over*weight?" Jejune scoffs, staring at the man in disbelief. "Have you seen the boy? He is so skinny I could blow him over with my breath."

"I'm overweight?" Stevey timidly cries, worriedly looking to me then Jejune.

Jejune leans down at Stevey and holds his face.

"No baby," she softly replies. "You are perfect." Jejune springs back up to the counter and begins riffling off to the man. "Listen I don't care what your little machine is telling you. He is fine the way he is so we'll gladly be adding the cookie to our order."

"I am sorry ma'am but he does not want to risk going over his maximum weight any –"

"You should be one to talk fatso!" Jejune snaps. "Why don't you wobble over to a scale and we'll await your number! I'm gonna guess you'll be *way* over your maximum weight," Jejune replies mockingly. They both stare at each other.

Just as the man is about to begin talking again, Jejune grabs a dish off the counter and whips it across the room. Silence covers the entire restaurant as everyone stops and follows the dish as it explodes off the wall. Stunned, the man's eyes stay glued to the wall. The man snaps his head back to Jejune infuriated.

"Ma'am I am going to have to –"

"Already one step ahead of you," she interrupts. "Come on Stevey let's go." Jejune gives the man one final glare before taking Stevey's hand and leaving the shop. I quickly mouth a sorry to the man before making my exit.

"Maximum weight. Maximum weight my ass, can you believe that crap," Jejune exasperates. Allowing Jejune to blow off some steam, I remain a few paces behind her. Jejune is silently shaking her head when a sniffle grabs both of our attentions.

"Hey," Jejune says. Stevey turns his head away as Jejune tries to look into his eyes. "Hey, look at me." Jejune turns his face towards her. "Open your eyes Stevey." He squeezes them tighter, straining his face in the process. "Baby open your eyes for me," Jejune asks softly, almost a whisper.

Stevey loosens the grip he has on his face, slowly opening his eyes. Jejune worriedly shifts her eyes back and forth looking at his.

"That man's not worth it." Jejune shakes her head. "He is not worth any of your tears or your sadness."

"Am I," Stevey looks down and mumbles. "Am I really overweight?"

"Is that what you're worried about?" Jejune lets out a short laugh and brushes his hair back. "No baby, not at all. You don't have to worry about that, and you don't have to worry about anything." Jejune takes her hand and lifts Stevey's chin, his glossy eyes looking into hers. "What do I always say?"

"No matter the time, no matter the day," Stevey says. "I will always have my big sister JJ," they both say together.

"That's right, don't ever forget that," Jejune says. Stevey sniffles again and adjusts his glasses. "Hey," Jejune smiles, pulling him in closer. "You know what I think you need." Jejune reaches into her back pocket, taking out a plastic wrapped sugar cookie. Stevey looks down, his face lighting up.

"Thank you JJ!" he exclaims, wrapping his skinny arms around her neck.

Jejune holds him, closing her eyes, taking in the moment. There aren't many moments in life when heartache can transform into heart warmth, but Jejune has a way of making any situation a good one, especially for Stevey.

Stevey takes the cookie and hastily unwraps it. Although we are all going back to their place, I hang back. I want them to enjoy this moment together a little longer. Holding hands, walking side by side, sharing a memory, and a stolen sugar cookie.

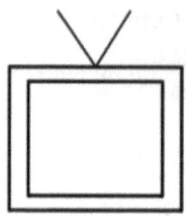

With the commotion Jejune caused at the shop, we made our own lunches once we arrived back at their place. Now as the day concludes, Stevey and I relax on the couch and watch television. My eyes focus on the time in the corner of the screen which reads 19:58.

"Hey Jejune," I yell over my shoulder. "Come join us." Jejune does not respond, only the faint running of the sink and occasional clinking of a plate let us know of her presence. "Jejune!" A plate slams on the counter in the kitchen.

"What," Jejune replies aggravated.

"The announcement is going to start."

"You know I don't listen to that shit," Jejune states, continuing to clean dishes. Stevey and I cover each other's ears, almost hitting one another in the face.

"That is not a nice word JJ," Stevey giggles out.

"Like I give a flying –"

Jejune is cut off as the small, worn down television changes to a white screen and the sound of six blaring short beats fill the room. Stevey and I unplug one another's ears and focus on the screen. Unfazed by the summoning sound, Jejune continues to clean dishes not even blinking. Stevey's tiny fingers tap my arm, jolting me back to the television.

"It's about to start," he says smiling.

The white screen dissolves to reveal a slender woman, with rosy cheeks, red hair, and a blue dress showing just a hint of cleavage; the actress from this morning's shoot. She smiles and the déjà vu begins.

"Hello, Northerners. Amella would like to wish a Happy Counting to you all…"

"Wow," Stevey says. "She's pretty."

"Stevey you say that every time," I laugh.

"That's because she's pretty every time!" Stevey hops off the couch, seated inches away from the screen.

"…mourning the death of others, crying from injury. But thanks to Amella there are no more tears and no more crying…"

The words from the screen fade away as I think back to this morning, holding the sound boom over her head, capturing her every syllable.

"…the more powerful we become."

The actress pauses to smile at the camera. A smile that is not hers, one pasted on her artificial face. If only listeners knew the truth. The truth I know.

"…less spheres you have the less quality life you…"

But she does not make her life seem "less great" with her smile and six spheres. That is why she is pretty as Stevey puts it. All I see is the girl once the cameras are off. The girl with her six spheres peeled away, revealing who she really is. A disgraceful two.

"…Keep your spheres and do not shed your tears. Happy Counting Northerners."

She flashes that fraud of a smile one last time, her face exchanged for the Amella logo. The screen flashes white, the six beats chime, and the television returns back to normal.

"Nice job Rose, you've really outdone yourself," Jejune says mockingly. "The sound quality was spot on."

"Wait," Stevey whips his head back, a huge smile on his face as he crawls onto the couch. "You know who that girl is!" Stevey happily asks.

"Yes I do," I reply.

"Is she as pretty as she is on television?" Stevey anxiously asks.

I scan over Stevey's face, excitement taking hold. If only he knew the truth. That what he just saw was a lie, and the actress does not look like that; she is a fake. Just like the actress, I fake a smile and lie through my teeth.

"She is even more pretty in person," I state. Stevey's smile grows even bigger, fanning over his petite face.

"Alright little man. Time for you to go to bed," Jejune says.

"No," he wines.

"No!" Jejune states as if in shock. Stevey lets out a giggle as Jejune grabs him from behind, breaking Stevey out of his dream like state. "Did you say no to me!" Stevey nods and Jejune begins to tickle him, laughter erupting from his mouth. "Say goodnight to Rose and thank her for spending the *whole* day with us," Jejune whispers in his ear. She releases her hold on Stevey and he collapses into my arms.

"Thank you for spending the day with me. I love you."

"I love you too Stevey," I reply. Stevey runs down the hallway towards his room, residing for the night.

"I really don't know how you do it," Jejune states.

"Do what?" I ask, even though I know where this conversation is heading.

"Work for them," she puts bluntly.

"A job is a job."

"But for Amella? For them?" I begin to chuckle. "What," she snaps back.

"You know, you technically work for Amella too," I scoff. "Amella runs everything."

"Like I don't already know that," Jejune states, sternly pointing to her hat and spheres on her face. "It's just... how can you work so close to the people that feed us lies." I never really saw it as I was feeding the lies, that I was contributing to the façade. I guess in some respect though, I am.

"I love my job," I slowly state back. "That does not mean I have to love the people." Jejune cradles her head in her hand as she slowly nods. "Well, I guess I should be heading out," I say, hoisting myself off the couch.

"Yeah, don't wanna get caught outside after curfew," Jejune says, rising off the couch with me. "If you're caught you'll get shot," she states, imitating the voice of the Amella actress. We both start to laugh at how terrible of an imitation that was.

"You get shot?" Our laughter ceases. I look past Jejune to see Stevey timidly standing in the doorway. "You get shot," he repeats, fear in his voice.

"Stevey," Jejune closes her eyes, opening them as she turns to face him. "Why are you still awake," she asks, crouching down to his level.

"Do people really shoot you?" he swallows, clenching his pajamas. "Like... with a gun?"

"Sometimes," Jejune pauses to gather her words. "Terrible people want to send–"

"Stevey can you spell that?" I excitedly ask.

"Spell what?" Stevey glances over Jejune's shoulder to meet my eyes.

"Terrible. I bet you cannot spell that word," I state with a smirk. Jejune looks back at me annoyed. If anyone is going to be the scapegoat for her hatred towards Amella it will be me, not Stevey.

"T.E.R.R.I.B.L.E." he rambles with a grin.

"Wow! You're gonna need some rest after that spelling. I'll race ya!" I chase Stevey to his room, purposefully falling behind to let him win.

"I win," he exclaims out of breath throwing himself on his bed.

"You are one fast runner." I heave over pretending to be wiped out. "Now, get some good sleep." I turn off his light and begin to close his door.

"Rose," he quietly asks.

"Yes Stevey?" I hold the door open, allowing the last bit of light to creep in to show his four spheres.

"Can you really get shot?" Stevey is biting his lower lip, concern in his expression. Just as I did earlier with the actress Stevey so truly loves, I fake a smile and lie through my teeth.

"No," I shake my head and let out a small laugh. "You know JJ, she has a crazy sense of humor."

"Ya," he chuckles as his teeth scrape across his lips to form a smile. "JJ is crazy."

"Goodnight Stevey." Closing the door, I wait a second as I depart back to the living room. I know Jejune, I know how she is going to react. Just as I pictured, Jejune is standing upright, arms crossed. Although her hat casts a shadow over her furious eyes, I can sense they are staring through me.

"I –"

"He has to learn," Jejune bluntly states, cutting me off.

"Learn," I repeat. "He is a *child* Jejune."

"You and I both know Stevey is much more intelligent than kids his age."

"He is just a boy," I plead, trying to make her understand. No matter how great at spelling or memorization Stevey is, it does not change how he views the world. He views his world with a lens of innocence, but in time, his lens will be shattered with the truth of the world, but the time to adjust his lens is not now.

"He has to know the truth," she states.

"It is not your place," I reply, trying to get it through to her.

"Then whose is it," Jejune exclaims, throwing her hands by her side. "You want him to hear his classmates talk about it. Overhear parents whispering about it. You want him to *see* it! An–an–and then what," Jejune continues to ramble, stumbling over her words. "Have Stevey be traumatized by that forever. No way, I'm not gonna feed him lies like you do to everyone else."

Jejune looks down, her hat shielding her face. Before I respond, she picks her head back up, eyes glossed over. In all my years of being Jejune's friend, I have never seen her get emotional to the point of tears.

"No," she repeats, holding back tears. "No, I can't let that happen. Not to him." Her brows twitch as she blinks rapidly, trying to capture the water in her emerald eyes from escaping onto her cheeks.

"You know," she continues, her voice quivering. "I can only control so much of his life, and *this* I want to have control over. Rose, you think we live in this perfect world but we don't." The bloodshot from her scar fixates on me, piercing through me like a knife. "So the little freedom that I have I will defend until my last breath, and I'll make sure Stevey is protected and loved." With a short sniffle, she composes herself, returning back to her statuesque pose. "So yes, for him to know the truth, it is my place."

The ability to love someone more than yourself is something I have never truly understood. Probably because I have not been given the chance to experience that feeling, but Jejune has. She has that love for Stevey, and it is not just because he is her younger brother, but because he is the younger brother of Amella as well. She does not like Amella and I can never figure out why. Amella protects us and we live a good life as long as we follow the rules. So yes, the love she has for Stevey is something I do not understand, but I appreciate it.

"Just do it right, okay? For him." Jejune gently nods. "I will show myself out." Walking past her frozen body, I grab my bag, open the door, and close it behind me. The door collides with the house, echoing in the silence of the North.

Jejune may be my best friend, but that does not mean that I agree with her. To be honest, we never agree on anything anymore, but we still need each other. Kind of like socks. Each come in a pair, even if you mismatch, it just does not quite feel the same. You need the pair to feel complete.

I hoist my backpack on my shoulders and begin my walk home. I have no clue what time it is, but I am guessing it is approaching curfew. I need to get home now, Amella is already surveilling the streets and taking its stand.

V. ANGELO

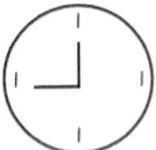

My eyes rapidly move with each step I take, noticing dark silhouettes disguised in the shadows. Night crew. I know curfew is not until nine o'clock, but it is as though they are stalking my every move to find something they can act on. I keep my head down fearful if I tilt my head ever so slightly in their direction, they will question me. What Jejune said earlier was true; if you get caught you'll get shot. What she was referring to was if you get caught outside after curfew. Once nine o'clock comes around, no one is outside, unless you have a death wish. I have heard stories. Shot in the head. Instant kill. For no one else to hear and, just like that, you are erased. No one talks about it either. If you do not see someone anymore, you do not ask questions, you just know. They are gone.

I continue my walk home. My neck begins to ache as I watch my feet move back and forth. Suddenly I hear the fast crunching of gravel and notice a handful of cars whizzing by me, their headlights disclosing my presence. Must be people trying to refill their spheres before curfew. I hope I never have to do that. Not only is the line so long but getting a refill on spheres is not cheap. I slump my neck back down and pick up my pace. I have no clue what time it is, but judging by how fast those cars were speeding, I am guessing it is close to curfew. I wish there was a clock somewhere but Amella does not allow public clocks; it is your responsibility to know.

Looking to my right, I vaguely notice where we filmed this morning. It was so chaotic and intense. People running, screaming at one another, equipment everywhere… and now, nothing. Just the sound of my heartbeat pounding in my ears and the steady melody of my shoes hitting the ground. Life moves on so quickly.

I walk a little further, passing by the restaurant where Jejune caused the commotion earlier, the weigh screens illuminating the dark space. Besides the light from inside the restaurant and occasional vein scanners placed throughout the streets, the North is pitch black. The restaurant is almost captivating with its artificial glow. My feet begin to turn my body down a side street, my neck still turned away to take one last look at the restaurant.

I wonder if the plate Jejune smashed is –

My body halts as it hits a wall, interrupting my thoughts. My cheek brushes up against the scratchy surface. My heart stops and my bones stiffen when I realize I did not crash into a wall. I bounce back from the collision and cautiously shift my eyes forward. I am confronted by a vest with six circles encompassing the word '*Amella*'.

"Watch it," a muffled voice says to me.

Like a lightning bolt, my gaze motions from the Amella logo, to the night crew's face, back to the Amella logo. From my brief glance, the crew member is in all black and wearing a face mask. Sheepishly, I nod my head and my brain knows to go but my feet are hesitant. The crew member firmly shoulders past me and his movement generates a flinch throughout my body allowing my feet to push me forward. When I feel as though I am far enough along, I peek over my shoulder.

His figure is monstrous, his camouflaged head held high and his shoulders pulled down as he grips a gun behind his back. I snap my head front. Night crew's favorite accessories: a mask and a gun. What a cowardly way to execute someone. You do not even get the satisfaction of knowing what your killer looks like. My heartbeat pounding in my ears subsides, along with the cementation of my bones.

'Watch it'. A simple watch it. I thought night crew was supposed to be frightening, chilling, even intimidating. Proving to us that we have to follow the rules and,

if not, they will eliminate people with one smooth curl of a finger without hesitation. That statement did not sound like a man who could do the unspeakable, but then again, it is not after curfew.

Finally in view, my house gets closer with each shaky step. Two houses over, I pick up my pace. Running may grab the attention of some night crew members concealed around me, but I am not thinking about that. I just want to make it home. Safe and sound before the stroke of nine.

Fumbling in my pocket for my key, the skin on my face bounces up and down with every leap to my house, almost in slow motion. My long strides turn into short scuffles as I reach my front door. Before I can turn the key, the knob twitches and the door wildly swings open revealing my mom, concern and distress washed over her face. Instantly her hand reaches for my arm, yanking me into the house. She seals the door shut and hastily wraps her arms around me.

"Where were you," she anxiously asks. I can barely reply as she clenches my back with such force. Her warm breath against my chilled ear is jittery, I must have really worried her.

"I was just walking home from Jejune's," I reply back.

"Just at Jejune's." She releases her grip over me, slowly opening her eyes to look at me head on. "Do you know what time it is?" My mom and I both know I do not know the answer to that question, but now is not the time to give her a snappy response.

"I am sorry," is all I can come up with. "But I am home now."

"What were you even doing over there so late?" Her boney fingers massage her head as she walks to the kitchen.

"We were watching the announcement," I firmly state back. She always compliments me on the sound quality from the announcements, but not tonight I guess. "I am gonna get to bed, got an early day tomorrow."

"We all do Rose," my mom exhales, still facing away from me.

I know the right thing to do is to turn around, say I am sorry, and give my mom a hug. But I am not in the mood for that. I will be spending enough quality time with her and my dad tomorrow for Counting Day. I love my mom but that does not mean I have to always like her.

I kick my shoes off and peel my clothes from my body. I lift my blanket to create a tsunami wave hovering above my bed, and as the wave of my sheets crash over me, the coolness of the fabric stings my body. As I lie awake in my now warm bed, I look over to the clock on my nightstand. Twenty one colon zero zero. Curfew. While I am secure inside my house some fool is out there stranded. Now they have to pay for it without even a chance to defend themselves; bullet to the head.

I wonder where that crew member is that I bumped into. Would he first say 'watch it' like he did to me and then pull the trigger? Does he have spheres like the rest of us or does his mask conceal more than just his voice? I know he is supposed to portray a man of fear but his voice, the simple 'watch it' response, I did not fear him after that. But I suppose people who do the unspeakable do not have the appearance of people who can do the unspeakable. Pushing my thoughts aside, I focus on sleep. I need to be well rested for tomorrow's Counting Day and in the right state of mind.

BANG! BANG! BANG!

Sporadically twitching my eyes open, I am illuminated with the same image every morning: dimly painted walls and slices of dusk entering my room through my curtains.

"Honey it's time!"

"I will miss you," I mumble into my bed. Like a band aid, I whip the covers off me. The cold air crawls over my body like baby spiders as I quickly rush to find pants and a shirt.

BANG! BANG! BANG!

"Rose, it's your –"

"Coming now!" I scream. Why do national events make everyone so insane? Exiting my room, I head towards the bathroom to get ready. Catching flies, my dad is out cold on the couch. It is not that he is lazy, he just works vigorously. I knock into his dangling arm giving him the motion of *wake up dad*. I hear the couch creek and I continue walking as he finally wakes up; mission accomplished.

After completing my morning routine, I emerge from the bathroom to see my dad once again sleeping on the couch but now in full Amella uniform of blue suit and tie. My mom continues to clean the kitchen in her house clothes. My dad's arm is once again hanging from the couch, practically begging me to make contact with it. I approach my dad's almost lifeless body, but my mission is stopped as I vaguely see hands waving frantically out of the corner of my eye.

"Just let your father rest until it's time," my mom whispers. "He was up all night and now he has to stay up all day. Your poor father hasn't gotten a break." I put my palms up to her in an "I'm sorry" motion and tiptoe away. "I'm about to change and then we can head out." I give a thumbs up and proceed to my room to finish getting ready.

Heading to my closet, I think about how much I dread this day. Using both hands, I forcefully move all my clothes over to reveal a tucked away garment bag. A blurry image of a bright blue blob protrudes from within the sheer bag. I gingerly remove the bag from its natural habitat and set the garment on the edge of my bed. Pulling down, I allow the zipper to glide across its teeth from top to bottom. The once hazy image becomes clear like that of steam being wiped away from a bathroom mirror to present my Counting Day uniform.

I strip down and begin taking the uniform off the hanger. My eyes focus as I again watch the tiny metal from the zipper glide across its teeth but this time on the back of my uniform. Pinching the top of the uniform, I carefully step into the garment and slide it up over my body. Struggling, I find the zipper and let it smoothly park just below the back of my neck. I close my closet door to see my twin in the mirror's reflection.

Revealing every curve, a royal blue pencil dress clings to my body while a dip in the front allows cleavage to peek out ever so subtly. Over my heart is Amella's logo of six white spheres encapsulating the stitching of *N. Amella* in cursive format, symbolizing I am from the North. I drag my palms across the dress, smoothing out the material across my body and down my sleeves. Perfection is of the utmost importance. No flaws. No mishaps.

BANG! BANG! BANG!

"Yup," I respond back. I grab my heels from the garment bag and briskly put them on. I take one last glance at my reflection before leaving my room, my feet clicking with each step.

"Oh Rose, you look stunning," my mom says, bringing her hands to her mouth in awe of my appearance. She does this every Counting Day.

"Thank you mom," I reply back, closing my bedroom door behind me. My eyes shift from my mom's glossed over eyes to my dad's drained eyes. The exhaustion in his eyes is replaced by joy as he spreads his arms out wide.

"Good morning my flower," he says. My heels click as I approach him. I am not a big fan of hugs but I love hugs from my dad, they make me feel safe. We release from our embrace, his eyes still filled with joy.

I follow my parents out the front door and direct my attention to the stampede of people outside. Identical in blue uniform, everyone is weaving in and out creating a spider web of motion. Although the state is shut down for Counting Day, the North is vibrant in color and movement.

"We should've left earlier," my mom says, shocked by how many people are out and about. She recites this phrase every time it is Counting Day. You would think by now she knows that everyone is flocking the streets.

For fear that people will attempt to flee during Counting Day, all individually controlled modes of transportation are not permitted on this day. That is Amella's fancy way of saying no one can drive on Counting Day. Luckily for my family, we are only an hour out from North Amella where Counting Day is held and a short walking distance to the trains. Some families however have to travel days even weeks in advance. The North, being such a huge landscape, has many Northerners taking boats to cross bodies of water or even hopping on airplanes to arrive.

As people hurry to the train station, you can spot the ones that do not belong. They are nervously following everyone else and seem lost in the sea of people. One family catches my attention as we all hustle to the station. A husband and wife firmly grasp tiny hands in each of their palms. I have never seen the parents or these children before around here, and they have that essence of just following everyone else, becoming the shadows of others surrounding them. They must have traveled far for this Counting Day judging by the exhaustion screaming off their faces.

"What do you think Henry?" my mom loudly asks, attempting to be heard over the herd of Northerners.

"Probably three or four minutes," he calmly replies.

"Okay I don't want to miss it."

"We never do Elle," my dad says, reaching for my mom's hand. "Relax." We could leave a fortnight before Counting Day and my mom would still be worried we would miss the train. Even if we missed the train, a new one arrives every five minutes, on the dot.

With a minute to spare for the next train arrival, we reach the station. Since this is a national event, fare is free for everyone. As we enter the station, the display board has the times of each train arriving under the caption HAPPY COUNTING DAY. Check in starts at 11:00 and this station allots forty five minutes for the train to arrive at North Amella. The display shows the times in ascending order, starting with the most recent train arrival at 9:45 all the way until 10:15. The 10:15 train is nicknamed the last stragglers since it is the final train to arrive to North Amella.

"Attention Northerners, the next train for North Amella is now approaching," an automated voice announces. With my ears focused on the sound of the train, my eyes look around to find any familiar faces. Jejune? Chard? Stevey? No luck. I give up my search and allow my eyes to correspond to the loud, monstrous piece of metal towers creeping into the station. Bulky, black figures are positioned in each doorframe leading into the train distorting the train's sleek, silver shine. Train crew. Unlike the night crew, a mask does not shield their faces, but rather, a gun shields their bodies.

An elongated hiss signifies to all that the train has come to a complete stop. We linger back and allow for others to board the train first. Most people want the lower level of the train so they can get off the fastest for check in, but my mom and I prefer the upper level of the train. Either way everyone will arrive at the same time, but one might as well enjoy the view along the way.

Piling into the train, my family and I make our way to the upper level. I grab the closest window seat I can and plop down, my mom and dad taking the section behind me. I glance around as more people find open seats. Various faces with various amounts of spheres fill the train. Some with three spheres. Some with five spheres. Sixes are sitting next to twos. Ones are sitting next to fours. Although we are all dressed in the same uniform, heading to the same destination, we do not share the same identification.

My eyes stop when I notice a petite woman across the aisle sitting a few rows behind me. With an empty seat next to her, an older gentleman approaches. She turns her head in his direction with a small grin on her face. Making eye contact with him, her grin disappears, and she turns her body away from him to stare out the window. Embarrassed, the man softly sits next to her and validates her actions by keeping his head down.

He is weak, she is strong. He is sad, she is happy. He has a bad life, she has a great life. I know this because, according to Amella, he is a one and she is a six. I would be ashamed to show my face in public with only one sphere, but I guess one should never judge a book by its cover or, in this case, a person by their spheres. Hitting his knee, the old man flinches his leg away from the aisle and looks up at the person apologetically. As he returns his gaze to its rightful place, he shyly scans the train and our eyes meet. Arctic blues and swirls of white interlock with my saturated brown eyes. Then he does something Amella would never dare think a person with one sphere could do. He smiles. A soft, pleasant smile.

The old man's flawless white teeth, combined with his stark white hair, bushy white eyebrows, and lively whites of his eyes radiate. I am fixated on him. A six engrossed with a one. His control over me is broken as more people make their way through the aisle. I blink and turn my head back front.

***

Nature is calm today. The leaves are dancing on the trees as the clouds sluggishly change their position in the sky. My window plays peek a boo with me as the train continues on to its destination. The hands of nature opening to see the sights of the North and closing over her eyes as I enter a tunnel, opening once again when I emerge. Not surprisingly, dad is passed out behind me as my mom is craning her neck like me to take in the sights. After a few stops and forty five minutes later, nature's landscape is replaced with North Amella.

The millions of leaves on trees are now millions of windows on buildings. The slow moving clouds are replaced by speeding transportation. Short houses, tall offices, skyscraper buildings, and not to mention the amount of people. One would think the streets are submerged in water at first glance. Upon closer examination, the water can be separated into hundreds of people dressed in blue. People walking, running, standing still. People entering and exiting buildings made of glass and mirrors. Fast buses, rapid trains, airplanes zigzagging. Clashes of blues, whites, silvers, and grays. It is organized chaos.

"Attention Northerners, we have arrived to North Amella. Happy Counting Day to all and good luck," the automated voice speaks again.

"Sleep well?" I ask my dad.

"Huh?" my dad says. "Oh me I wasn't sleeping. I was just resting my eyes." My mom and I roll our eyes as this is a comeback we have heard many times before.

I take one last look across the aisle for the old man who smiled at me before exiting the train, but he seems to have already left. Maneuvering among the crowd of people, we make our way off the packed train to check in.

"Boo!" I hear from behind me as two hands quickly jab my sides. Reacting, I jump a little bit. "Gotcha," Jejune says pointing finger guns at me. Being in heels with a slim fitting dress looking exactly like every other female present, Jejune still manages to seem misplaced.

"Wow Jejune, I don't think I have ever seen you in a dress," my mom says with a smile.

"Oh enjoy it while it last Mrs. Pharl, this only happens once a month."

"Well you look beautiful Jejune, very lady like."

"Thank you, but soon I get to strip down and show off my birthday suit," Jejune softly remarks for only me to hear, making a pelvic thrust motion.

"Stop that!" I say, slapping her to quit it. I guess we are all recovered from last night's incident, no hard feelings. "Where is Stevey?" Jejune motions behind me where he and my dad are talking. His wavy blonde hair is neatly parted and slicked back, he truly does look like a little man.

"I think we caught the train right after you guys, no last stragglers this month," she says. Although it is Counting Day, one of the most important days to behave in accordance with Amella standards, Jejune is still wearing one of her "screw you" hats. Keeping with the theme, her baseball cap is a royal blue color with the embroidery in a striking white. Six short chimes silence everyone outside check in.

"Hello Northerners," a calming voice blares overhead. "Amella would like to wish a Happy Counting Day to you all. Today marks Counting number five of this year. Check in will begin now and last until ten minutes after eleven. After that time, check in will be closed. Good luck and Happy Counting Northerners."

"Woo!" Jejune yells as people begin to check in. I slap her on the arm again. "What?" she laughs. "I'm excited."

The mixture of people mumbling and sporadic beeping of metal detectors is right on cue. Let the long day of counting begin.

V. ANGELO

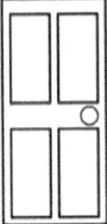

Throughout Counting Day, everyone completes a number of tests and exams. After passing check in, the tests begin. For objective reasons, every individual is judged on a scoring system. One point is granted for passing and zero points are given for failing and every point received in sections of the exams is equivalent to 100 points. The total number of points one can receive is eighteen hundred points, but I have yet to see that happen. Once everyone is tested, judged, and examined, points are all tallied. The total number of points is representative of your region. For us, we are the North competing against the States and the rest of the world.

The nonstop blaring of the metal detectors becomes increasingly louder as I approach the rectangular archways. Every Counting Day since I was young, I have tried to count the number of metal detectors that barricade North Amella but it is utterly impossible. Hundreds is my guess, and the same goes for crew members. The abundance of security is extreme. Amella's motive is to instill fear so no one attempts anything on this national day, and in my eyes, their mission is accomplished. Who would want to try anything when a deadly weapon can be spotted at every vantage point? With only a handful of people ahead of me, my family, Jejune, and Stevey go our separate ways to enter through the detectors.

"See you on the other side," Jejune says, taking Stevey's hand as they walk to the detector next to mine. My mom and dad take the one to my other side as I watch the rest of the people in front of me enter North Amella.

SPHERES

The first person in my line puts their arms up and walks through. The metal detector beeps as they pass through and I take a step forward. The next person puts their arms up and walks through. Beep. I take a step forward. I raise my arms up above my head. I have nothing to hide, but I always get that feeling that the detector will alert the crew I do have something to hide. An irrational fear, but when someone is holding an automatic weapon inches away from you, I think you have a right to be frightened. I enter the metal arch, leaving Northern territory and arriving in North Amella territory. Beep. My fear falls away as I bring my arms back down.

I make my way to the next test: pat down. Trying to keep my balance, I attempt to gracefully take my heels off. Reaching the crew member, I place my shoes by my side, spread my legs, and shoot my arms out making a starfish stance. The cloth from their black gloves glides up and down my bare legs, gently taps my hips and ribs, and finishes by sliding up and down my arms. With no response, I am signaled that I am clear. I jump into my heels and as the crew member moves to let me pass, North Amella is unveiled.

Sheets of glass are stacked on top of one another to form a skyscraper of beauty. Made of complete glass, North Amella's interior shines through to the outside world. Swirling marble and crystal chandeliers remind us all of just how amazing this day is and how fantastic Amella is. Hoisting myself up the ginormous pearl marble steps to North Amella, we all reunite. Stevey is holding Jejune's hand as she adjusts her hat the crew member made her remove. My mom and dad reach my side as we all make our journey to the sleek building. Crew members are lining the perimeters of the stairs, no one could escape even if they tried.

After the long ascent up the stairs, we all reach the clearing and make another venture towards the front doors. With a body width of separation, more Amella crew members are accompanying the last step of check in. We all make a single row, each standing in front of a different crew member and, in unison, we roll up our right sleeve and place our naked wrist on the vein scanner. The tiny computerized square is warm to the touch from all the wrists that have been placed there today.

Rather than use photographic identification or written documentation, vein scans are seen as much more efficient for keeping track of individuals who enter the building. Anyone can make a fake ID or forge a signature, but who would go so far as to cut off their arm to give their veins to another. A soft click notifies me that my vein scan is cleared.

"Rose Pharl number eight zero zero two," the crew member states.

"Thank you," I respond, rolling my sleeve back down.

Finally within North Amella's walls, we all linger in the semi circle lobby. The long hallways branching outward from the lobby make the building resemble shooting rays from the sun. Adding to Amella's beauty, two glass floating staircases curve to meet on the second floor. Citizens are only allowed on the first floor for Counting Day which is established by the high number of crew members lining the reflective stairs and second floor balcony.

"What do they have to hide?" Jejune asks as she steps next to me. "I mean this much security, it's almost unnecessary," she whispers, her eyes scanning all around us. "Anyways, eight thousands?"

"Eight thousand and two to be exact." Jejune and I exchange a smile as we wait for our numbers to be called. My mom and dad stand next to us and my mom grabs for my hand.

"Numbers seven nine nine nine through eight zero zero nine may proceed to hallway three," an automated voice declares in the lobby.

Making her way to hallway three, my mom's clammy fingers graze across my knuckles as she releases her grip and I follow in her shadow. The commotion from the lobby vanishes as myself, my parents, Jejune, Stevey, and five other Northerners make our way down the narrow white cocoon of a hallway. Like a tone deaf school music concert, the sound from our shoes clash as we all make our way down the echoing path. The continuous white setting is broken by crew members dressed in black once again accompanying vein scanners.

"Judgment day, judgment day," Jejune mumbles in front of me in a harmonious tune. All ten of us line up in front of a crew member. This moment is when Counting Day officially starts and the judgment begins. We are first judged on our appearance, specifically attire. A total of six hundred points can be earned in this section. Before the exam begins, another vein check is put in place, just in case someone wanted to switch identities with another while waiting in the lobby. Each of us follow the same procedure but we are not allowed to acknowledge or interact with any of the other nine individuals we are with.

I rest my wrist on the scanner, there is a short click, and I roll my sleeve back down. The crew member begins their process as they do every Counting Day. Naked eye, they scan over my dress looking for any loose threads, snags, or holes. I follow the crew member's eyes as they carefully trace the outline of my body. Arms, shoulders, breasts, hips, the crew member circles around me, as if observing a rare artifact in a glass case. They make sure my dress is not too small, too big, is the correct knee length, correct wrist length; nothing can be at fault.

Next is shoes. No scuffs, no holes, and the perfect amount of shine. The crew member takes out a color swatch and crouches down to compare the pigment quality. The same is done for my dress with a cloth swatch. After a thorough examination, the crew member steps back, waiting for the other nine Northerners to be surveyed. With all the crew members back in their formation, the solid wall behind them is severed by ten rectangular openings.

As we walk forward into our individual rooms, Jejune and I trade a glance before our separation. She pulls her hat back slightly mouthing the words 'birthday suit' with a wink. Smirking, I advance to my room, leaving Jejune's company of humor in the hallway. Once in my individual room, the slit in the wall becomes whole again. Retaining the sleekness of the building, chalk white walls cover the ten by ten cubical of a room. A slight breeze alerts me that the doctor has entered and I am to begin the second round of judgment: body. A total of four hundred points can be earned here.

"Please take a seat on the exam table," the doctor states.

I hop up on the exam table as my heeled feet dangle like a wind chime. The doctor finishes putting on her latex gloves and approaches my statuesque body. The warm breath from her nostrils pushes against my face as the sticky glove plasters my hair. This is done to make sure my hair does not exceed maximum length. Satisfied, she hastily removes her gloves.

"Undress please." She faces away to dispose of her gloves. This is my least favorite part of the exam, what Jejune calls the 'birthday suit'. It is not so much as I do not like to be bare in front of a complete stranger, but the individual rooms are always so cold. The chillness of the room attacks my body as I slip out of my heels and dress. "Step onto the scale."

My feet sting as they step on what feels like a block of ice. Just like at the restaurant where Jejune had her episode, the light from the scale reflects off my eyes. One one nine point three flashes on the screen which is the same as yesterday; no surprise. I step off the scale and the doctor has a new pair of gloves holding a disinfectant cloth. Just as my body was adjusting to the room temperature, I am bitten by the cold cloth as she aggressively wipes the inside of my elbow. Using her other hand, she clamps my arm and reaches on the counter for the needle. Without warning she injects the needle into my arm, and looking over her shoulder just in time, I avoid seeing the needle disappear into my skin to take a sample of my blood. The needle reappears from within my skin as she pulls the needle back, slaps the tube on the counter, and uses another cloth to put pressure on where the needle was. Through all this intimate interaction, she does not make eye contact with me, completely ignoring my nude presence.

"You may put your clothes back on," she states. Crawling back into my dress and shoes, I watch as the doctor adds a sticker to the test tube full of my blood. "You can take a seat back on the exam table once dressed."

Quietly, I pivot my body and glue my butt back on the exam table. I strain my eyes to look as far over without moving my head in her direction. She is placing the now deep red test tube into its holder and opens a drawer. After grabbing what she needs, she slams the cabinet and the noise knocks my eyes back forward.

"Look up please." I tilt my head back and straighten my spine. My eyes are locked with hers but she is looking down as she opens the facial wipes. "Close your eyes please," she states, continuing to open the wipe.

I take one last look at her not acknowledging me and close my eyes. My face becomes dough like as she meticulously drags the wipe up and down my face. This portion of the exam is to remove any makeup that may be covering imperfections such as scars, cuts, or pimples. It is also used to wipe off anyone trying to add extra spheres under their eyes. Amella has truly thought of everything. The doctor finally makes it to my spheres. The wipe skids across my skin, her fingers rising slightly as she reaches each sphere which stay secure to my face. If I did not have six spheres, it would never cross my mind to create fake ones. The consequences would be too severe. With my eyes still closed I can hear her get up to throw away the wipe and remove her plastic gloves. I keep my eyes closed for the final part of this exam.

Resembling a tiny flashlight, an infrared light is produced that scans each sphere. I do not really know how it identifies if a sphere is real or fake. Possibly for skin particles? Cells? Whatever may be the case she clicks the flashlight on one sphere, clicks the device off, and then clicks the device back on to flash on the next sphere. The motion of clicking on and off between each sphere is done for all six of mine. She reaches my last sphere, allowing the infrared light to bleed through my skin and clicks the flashlight off permanently.

"A crew member will escort you to your next room," the doctor states. I open my eyes, blinking a few times to adjust to the brightness. The rectangular opening appears again and a crew member is already positioned for my arrival. "Six," the doctor tells the crew member. The crew member nods and I follow their lead.

The squishy, firm boots of the crew members are in battle with the women's delicate clicking of heels and gentle scuffing of the men's dress shoes. The end result sounds like piles of silverware being dumped into an empty sink. Located in this hallway is where all the corresponding numbered rooms lead to your ballroom. Similar to aisles in a grocery store, I have hallways on my right increasing in number, along with doorways to my left increasing in number. We pass a row of doors labeled one, for all the Northerners with one sphere. After some time we stop and I turn to my left to see a gray door with the number six above.

"Scan your vein and enter," the crew member states.

Once again, I roll up my sleeve and place my wrist on the scanner. Unlike the time when entering the building, the surface of this scanner is cold. Once signaled all clear, I push open the gray door and am consumed by darkness. The door clicks behind me, locking me in and leaving me in the pitch dark. I have gathered throughout the years that this room is the size of a small closet. The first time in this room, my mom warned me that I would feel very confined in the space. To test this, I put my arms out but they stopped short of letting me straighten them. Although I found solid walls all around, they were covered with velvet curtains.

Standing in the dark, a square screen in front of me flashes on, monopolizing the darkness of the room. Amella's logo reflects off my eyes followed by my Counting Day results. Rose Pharl is at the top with my categories and scores next to each. My eyes move from the top of the list to the bottom as I scan my results.

The first section under appearance is dress.

Stitching: one hundred points.

Fit: one hundred points.

Color: one hundred points.

The second section is shoes.

Scuff: one hundred points.

Fit: one hundred points.

Color: one hundred points.

Next is my body exam.

Hair: one hundred points.

Weight: one hundred points.

Face: one hundred points.

Blood: one hundred points.

Last is my personal exam.

Spheres: six hundred points. You receive one hundred points for each sphere you hold.

Work: one hundred points. Which is not surprising because I was never late or called out of work this term.

Crime: zero points. My eyes stop.

Zero points? My eyes shift over to the comments section on how this could be because I have not committed any crimes. I read the following statement and am in disbelief: *Bystander to violent actions.*

Are they serious? *Bystander to violent actions* I read again. As in yesterday when Jejune threw the plate? That is far from violent actions. Blinking away my frustration, I click on SUBMIT at the bottom of the screen. Exhaling, I wait for my account to appear on the screen. My current point balance upon arrival is five thousand two hundred and the points I earned this Counting Day are one thousand seven hundred, just shy of a perfect score. Of my combined seventeen hundred points, I put four hundred in my travel account, four hundred in my food account, four hundred in my vacation time account, and the last five hundred in my miscellaneous account. My vacation account currently has the most points. I rarely take time off of work, but you never know, I may want to venture somewhere one day.

Satisfied with my division of points, I once again click on SUBMIT and six short chimes sing as Amella's logo fades onto the screen. The sixth chime is followed by darkness as the screen goes black, but is soon replaced with lively energy as the wall in front of me splits open, revealing the six ballroom.

Ivory, round tables are illuminated by dimly lit chandeliers. People mill about, some with drinks in hand standing and talking, while others huddle over tables laughing. The atmosphere is bubbly yet somber, like a sunny day being masked by heavy rain. This is the six ballroom. Every person in North Amella that has six spheres belongs in the six ballroom. This is the last event of Counting Day. Although the ballroom is filled with delicious smells from the food, feel good music, and breathtaking arrangements, I speak to no one as I make my way to the bar. My parents are not here. Jejune is not here. I keep to myself and order an ice cold water, quenching my thirst as I turn my attention to the stage and listen to the playing of smooth jazz.

"I never thought you as a jazz girl," a voice says behind me. I turn quickly to see Chard. "I'm more of an upbeat kind of guy." I nod and make a sound to show interest as I sip my water. "Ah, good ole water," Chard remarks pointing to my cup. "H_2O is the way to go," he states, slipping his hand back in his pocket.

"Could not agree with you more," I reply, removing the glass from my lips.

"I'm surprised by the amount of people." Chard swivels his body to see the crowd. "Either everyone is refilling their spheres, or less and less people are crying," he spits out with a smirk.

"I would like to think –" my thought is cut off as people clap at the conclusion of the song. The musicians bow, leaving one pianist on stage. The six spheres under his eyes glow from the brightness of the white keys as he creates faint background music.

"I'm actually glad I caught you," Chard says, taking a swig from his bottle before finishing his statement. "I was going to ask if you were working the North Amella shoot."

"North Amella shoot?"

"Amella wants each State to create promotional videos to get people to move to their State. They are asking the best of the best for crew members. If I remember correctly, little miss over here hasn't missed a day of work," he states, raising his eyebrows.

"You would be correct," I chuckle. "But it will be like every other announcement we make. What is so special that they have to select crew members?"

"We get to film here." Chard grins, making a gesture to the area around us.

"Here," I raise my eyebrows in surprise. "At North Amella?"

"Yup," Chard nods. "Pretty sweet right." He takes another swig from his bottle. "No one is allowed within these walls with the exception of Counting Day. I can't imagine being in this building on any other day." The pianist hits his last key and is met with the sound of faint claps. He takes a bow and leaves to go backstage. "Sit with me?" Although I do not want to spend the whole ceremony with Chard, no one else I know is a six. He is the only Northerner I know in this ballroom. Being the best option, we find two seats still with a great view of the stage. I settle my drink down and Chard pulls my chair out for me.

"Thank you," I say, brushing my dress underneath me. He smiles and takes the seat next to mine. I take a sip of my water and look around. The seating area is quiet compared to the loud colors on the stage. Spotlights and backlights punch the stage, a mix of whites, blues, and purples. It is truly spectacular as shadows of the piano, music stands, and other instruments line the back of the stage.

Murmurs start to fade as short clicks from high heels surround the ballroom.

As she crosses the stage and flashes her wall of perfect teeth, people sporadically begin to stand and applaud. The ceremony is starting. I join the noise making, watching as people's faces elate with joy. I sit back in my chair and I am taken aback. It is her, the actress just like she was at yesterday's shoot. Auburn, pixie hair. Round, baby blue eyes. Red butterfly lips. Royal blue pencil dress.

"Is that the actress from yesterday's shoot?" I whisper to Chard.

"Maybe," he whispers back with a shoulder shrug.

It looks just like her.

"Hello, Northerners. Amella would like to wish a Happy Thirty Sixth Hundredth Counting to you all," her voice projects, filling the room from the microphone on her face. Applause erupts again as her face floats on screens positioned on either side of the stage for the people sitting in the far back of the ballroom.

But it does not sound like her.

"And let us give a hand for our lovely music tonight." The actress motions to a table towards the edge of the stage. The musicians turn and wave in appreciation as people applaud once again.

I wonder what this actress really looks like.

"Amella would like to thank you all for being here today, we would not be one of the strongest States without our sixes."

I wonder if she is a six, or maybe she is a two like the actress yesterday.

"We will now be serving dinner. Please enjoy." The actress gives one last smile and chatter begins to fill the room once again. I watch as the actress makes her way off the stage and disappears behind the velvet curtains.

*** *

Fish, pasta, vegetables, fruit, rice. The variety of food present is ridiculous, and on Counting Day we do not have to worry about how much we eat. Weigh in

46

stations are voided; it is like our reward from Amella for being sixes. As we eat dinner, Chard and I get to know the others sitting at our table. The lady next to Chard is trying to get to know him a little bit more than anyone else. One works in the Construction Industry, one the Space Industry like my dad, and another in the Food Industry. Chard and I, being the youngest at the table, cannot relate to most of the conversation topics. As the waiters go around and take people's plates, the construction worker finally asks about Chard and I.

"So, what Industry do you guys work for?"

"Film," we both reply at the same time.

"Oh wow," the flirtatious lady sitting next to Chard says sipping her wine. "That's amazing." She inches her chair closer to Chard's.

"That's the one job I could not do," the construction worker chuckles.

"It is not that bad," I state.

"I love it," Chard chimes in.

"Oh, I bet you're good at what you do," the lady breathes, nearly spilling her drink as she tries to play with Chard's hair.

"Yeah." Chard leans onto the table to dodge her. "So good that we both may be filming here at North Amella." The whole table stops and the lady raises her eyebrows slumping back in her chair. A few of the men sip their drinks with wandering eyes as Chard and I exchange a quick glance. "I'm sorry, did I say something to offend anyone?"

"Oh no honey," the lady laughs, flagging a waiter for more wine. "I think we are just all surprised they would let workers as young as you come into this place." Chard starts to laugh as a hint of confusion crosses his face.

"How young do you think we are?" he scoffs. No one answers for a while, but then the drunk decides to speak again. With much effort, she pushes her body off from the chair to get closer to Chard.

"Well, not old enough to drink what you're drinking." She drunkenly bops her head around the table, looking for reassurance.

"At least we can handle what we are drinking," I remark. The lady stops gazing at Chard's face and slumps back, erasing her thoughts of seduction.

"You going to let your girlfriend talk to another woman like that!" she exclaims, pointing a deflated finger at me.

"Oh no, she is not –"

"Where is the dumb waiter with my drink!" The lady bangs on the table ceasing Chard's response. Tables around us glimpse in our direction, exchanging hushed comments. "Well anyway," she sloppily says, her eyelids getting heavy. "When you do film here," she pauses to get the very last drop from her glass, throwing her head back dramatically. "When you do film here, make sure to tell Veil that Sasha says hi." She plops the empty glass on the table and staggers to reach Chard's ear. "And I miss our late nights together," she whispers with a weighted breath. Chard twitches away as she reclines back with a drunken smirk. The lining of her dress creeps up her thighs as she spreads her legs and Chard and I look away in embarrassment.

"Nice table you picked," I mumble.

"Hey," the construction worker spits out across the table. Chard and I revert our eyes to him, his six spheres piercing towards mine. "A word of advice," he looks towards the drunk I now know is named Sasha, softly breathing in and out as she takes her well needed nap. "If you do see Veil, best not to say anything."

Before I am able to respond, the actress walks back onto the stage, applause erupting from every corner of the ballroom. The construction worker gives us both a quick nod before turning away to face the stage. Chard and I look at one another, a mix of confusion and creepiness filling my body. Veil? Who's Veil? To not draw any attention our way, we too face the stage and begin clapping, joining the other sixes around us.

"My, this is going to turn into Counting Night if we clap every time someone comes on stage!" the actress shouts, her white teeth beaming as people in the ballroom begin to laugh with her in amusement. "Once again, thank you all for being here and most importantly for being sixes." As the actress continues her speech, the lights on the stage transform to shades of deep teal and amethyst as a giant screen slowly slides down behind her. "Here in the North, we pride ourselves on our confidence and strength. Others, such as ones and twos, look up to us, the sixes, to achieve those types of qualities. Most importantly, we pride ourselves on how we properly present ourselves to others."

"Yeah," I snicker looking towards Sasha. "She really presents herself properly," I mumble just for Chard to hear. He forms a quick smirk. Chard and I may not be the best of friends, but I am glad we share the same sense of humor.

"And now," the actress continues. "It is my pleasure to reveal this Counting Day's World results." The ballroom becomes dead silent. Everyone gazes at the stark white screen waiting for the results, the screen reflecting off the whites of our eyes and whites of our spheres.

The results emerge but my view of the stage is blocked as people stand. You can tell who has had a little too much to drink due to the ones hooting and hollering. I attempt to peer through the crowd as if I am looking through a shrub consumed by leaves but the others around me obscure my view.

Finally, my eyes revert to the screen on the side of the stage. The North takes the lead once again with India a close second and the list continues for the rest of the World's States and Countries. I stare at Chard, his ocean blue eyes and large nose looking at me.

SPHERES

"The best of the best," he shouts. My palms begin to move towards each other to join in filling the large ballroom with noise when a lightning strike of fear runs head to toe through my body, stopping my hands from coming together. The exhilaration of everyone is shushed by the short whistle of a gun.

Humans are a fascinating species. We walk upright on both legs, speak a multitude of languages, and possess an array of special talents. Some humans are great at memorization, others athletic abilities, and many are musically inclined. But the most captivating of all is when you realize humans can do something that you never thought possible. Such as a human producing a shriek so piercing that just the sound screams pure terror.

As if the floor below everyone disappeared, royal blue figures in front of me nervously descend, allowing a full view of the stage. I witness the final movements of the actress' lifeless body resembling someone sinking to the bottom of the ocean. Her arms and legs sway to the right as her stomach pulls her body down in the opposite direction to the floor. Unlike her gracefulness throughout the ceremony, her contact with the stage floor creates a deep thud.

Her auburn, pixie hair compliments the blood spreading on the stage. Her dead, baby blue eyes hypnotize as static red lips separate to display a face of pain. The dip in the front of her dress allows the entrance of the bullet to peek out ever so subtly. She is still captivating, but not in the way she is supposed to be. Panic and horror continue to fill the ballroom. People are crawling under tables, holding one another for comfort, doing anything to believe they are safe. Thankfully, the North's young citizens, including toddlers and children, are in a separate ballroom away from all this hysteria.

"Rose!" A stampede of footsteps echo behind me. I turn to see crew members bolting to the stage, determination in their strides. "Rose! Get down!" Chard grabs my waist, forcing me to the ground.

I stumble to the floor as Chard and I watch crew members zigzag through fallen chairs and frightened people to get to the stage. I free from Chard's hold on me and peer over the table. My eyes sporadically move back and forth to look at the abundance of crew members. I look back to the stage where the actress rests in a pool of her own blood, then to the person behind this ruthless act.

Tears fill the man's eyes as he regretfully turns away from the actress. He timidly lowers his arm from the position it was in when he took the shot. It is him. The old man I saw on the train. My eyes widen at the sight of him standing up on stage with a gun in his hand, his saddened face looking out to the petrified ballroom. I know this is not going to end well, but I continue to watch it all unfold, because that is what intrigues people most, witnessing something you know is wrong but you still cannot turn away.

The man sternly lifts his chin, gazing up at the lights shining on him. Tears stream down his cheeks as his final sphere evaporates from his face and there are no more spheres to be lost under his eyes. Without hesitation he connects the gun to his head and pulls the trigger. Before I can look away, everything goes black.

My eardrums fill with what sounds like an enormous rainstorm. Dense rain drops relentlessly pounding against hard metal. I duck behind the table and squeeze my hands over my ears as Amella's crew members continuously shoot in the dark. I have never been this scared in my life. I flinch as I feel hands frantically tapping at me and uncover my ears, reaching back to stop the motion.

"I'm here! I'm here!" I scream to Chard.

"Rose we can't stay here!" Chard hollers back. My eyes move back and forth trying to make out Chard in front of me, but I can see absolutely nothing. The firing of Amella's guns continues to blare, drowning out the cries of fear in the ballroom.

"There's nowhere to go!" My body starts to tremble. My heartbeat pulsates in my head as I breathe rapidly. Pressure emerges behind my eyes and the top of my nose. The sensation is something I have never felt before. "I don't want to die," I timidly project. The pressure behind my eyes continues to build. Is this what it feels like to cry?

"You won't die," Chard firmly states, fumbling to make contact with my arm. "Okay?" A rush of warmth relaxes my stressed bones as Chard caresses my frightened body. I nod in agreement trying to blink away this foreign feeling filling my face. Realizing he can't see my motion, I reply with a simple okay.

The firing of bullets subsides as what feels like an earthquake shakes underneath the ballroom. Although I can't see, I feel the breeze of people running by. Are they retreating? After a few seconds all the lights in the ballroom come back on. Chard is inches away from my face still grasping my arm. I rapidly look around to take in my surroundings of broken plates, over turned chairs, and smashed food; the place is a mess.

"You alright?" Chard asks, worry in his eyes.

"Yeah I'm alright," I shyly say back. The tension in my face washes away. My bones start to relax. Chard releases his hold on my arm as we both look around and gather our bearings. He checks in with the people who were sitting at our table, even assisting Sasha after she tried to get in his pants all night. Still shaken, I stay situated on the ground. Did this really just happen?

A woman abruptly crawls out from underneath a neighboring table. Her dress is lopsided and her heels have fallen off. She emerges with damp cheeks and takes in her surroundings just like myself. Her damp cheeks should have been a giveaway, but I think I was in too much shock to realize at first. The woman sniffles as her eyes, now with only five spheres, scan the ballroom. I immediately drag my shaky fingers under my eyes for reassurance, feeling the number of bumps. Six. I still have six. The woman weakly collapses to the floor, continuing to sob. She came to this ballroom a six and now she is leaving a five. As I continue to see the aftermath of this unexpected event, there are many sixes who are now fives, but I don't blame her or anyone else for crying. We've all just experienced a traumatic incident, I was on the verge of tears myself.

Thinking of tears, I revert my attention from the crying woman on the floor to the man who was crying on stage. I use the table for leverage to get up but I stop myself. I saw him put the gun to his head, but I don't know if he shot himself or the crew members finished the job. Either way, the aftermath of the outcome is going to be sprawled across the ballroom's vibrantly lit stage. I brace myself for the image I may see.

I help myself up off the ground and the stage is just how it was before. Music stands, blue and purple lights, the screen reporting the World results, but there is no actress floating above a pool of blood or the aftermath of an old man committing suicide. The stage remains untouched; disbelief crosses my face. The ballroom looks as though a tornado destroyed everything but the stage. A crew member hops onto the stage, the black of his uniform sucking in the lights. He peels off his black mask and the sweat dripping from his face glistens.

"Attention!" the crew member yells from his wide mouth, silencing the ballroom's hysteria. "We are evacuating North Amella at this time." His automatic firearm rests across his strongly built body. "If you are in need of medical attention, please stay where you are. If you are capable of leaving, please do so now." A handful of people begin to adjust their attire and head for the doors. How can they be so calm? "We are considering this an act of terrorism," the crew member firmly states. "Amella will be handling the events that have happened here and report to the public in a short time. All will be resolved and there is no need to worry." The crew member nods to signify the conclusion of his announcement, his boots scuffing as he makes his way to the edge of the stage, walking past the spot where a dead old man should be.

"I'm going to stay and see if anyone needs help," Chard says to me. "Will you be okay going by yourself?" I look at Chard in disgust.

"You saw them right?"

"Saw who?" he replies, confusion in his face.

"The girl on stage and the old man. He killed her."

"I heard a gunshot but –"

"But you saw them," I ask again.

"The actress on the stage? Yes I saw her," Chard states, his confusion unfazed.

"Then where did she go?" I ask sincerely. Chard looks to the stage with an open mouth, searching for what to say.

"I don't know Rose. Everything went dark and I ducked for cover. Now are you going to be okay if I stay here?" Why is he not concerned about this? Why didn't he see what I saw?

"I will be fine on my own." With a hint of aggravation, I march towards an exit. Lost for words, Chard attempts to continue the conversation but turns to helping those around him as I walk away.

What the fuck is going on?

Walking as if I'm on eggshells, I maneuver my way around the demolished ballroom and take one last look at the stage. Nothing. No evidence of there ever being two dead bodies there, let alone in the last five minutes. I head for the door but a hand presses up against my shoulder. I am met face to face with an Amella crew member, they stare at me for some time and I stare back.

"Go," he mumbles under his mask. Before leaving the ballroom, I look to my left. There are a pack of Northerners huddled together, all of who are either crying hysterically or without the six spheres they came here with.

Not wanting to refuse the crew member's order, I make my way through the doorway leaving the ballroom behind me. Following the crowd, I exit the building as everyone is calm and unnerved, as if a major shoot out didn't just occur. As I am leaving, I notice a number of camera crews lining the hallways and lobby. Although tempting to stare into the reflective lens, I keep my head down and continue my way out the door. Still shaken, I make it outside the metal detectors and reach my parents who look ecstatic.

"What kind of entertainment did your ballroom have this time?" my mom asks enthusiastically. "Your father and I's ballroom had some entertainment, but it sounded like you guys were having a great time with all the shouting and rock music." Unfazed by my mom's comments, I look around to see anyone feeling the same as me. I see sixes shedding tears as family members comfort them in confusion, sixes frantically speaking to random strangers, and other sixes just having a look of shock as they make their way to the trains.

"Honey," my mom says as I continue craning my neck to take in the surrounding six's reactions. "Rose are you alright?" I snap out of it and look to my parents who are both waiting for a response.

"Music? Mom, those were gun shots. A woman was murdered. Why do you think everyone is leaving."

"What?" I can feel the tension of her body colliding with mine as she squeezes me tight. My dad rubs her back for support. "What do you mean a woman was murdered?" she frantically asks over my shoulder.

"We need to leave," my dad states. He stops rubbing my mom's back and gently hoists her off me. "Now. It's not safe here." My dad begins walking back towards the train as my mom and I follow. I can see the concern on my mom's face.

"Mom I am okay," I reassure her. "Just hold it in."

"Hold it in," she scoffs. "You're my daughter Rose, it would be unnatural for me not to be upset." Before I step on the train my dad grabs my shoulder so I can face him. He quickly looks at the crew member standing in the door then back at me.

"You are strong my flower." He kisses me on the forehead and heads onto the train.

SPHERES

Once we are home behind closed doors, I tell my parents everything. The actress, the old man, the black out, the bodies disappearing. My mom and I sit across from one another on the couch, still in our Counting Day uniforms while my dad is in the bathroom changing for work. He leaves the door open as I relay the events.

"Henry," my mom says, interrupting my story and rising from the couch. "I don't want you to go." The bathroom goes dark as my dad flicks the light off.

"I have to, you know that," he replies, heading towards the kitchen.

"I'll be worried all night," my mom states, following his path.

"I'll be fine." My dad closes the fridge and approaches my mom. "Elle, what happened today has nothing to do with any of us. If anything happens, I will call." He gives my mom a kiss.

My mom returns back to the living room, closing her eyes to keep the tears in. She puts her head in her hands as she sinks back into the couch. I look up towards my dad and nod to let him know I will watch her. Amella is meant to wash out any negative emotions we may have, yet my mom still has them.

"I'll be back in the morning." My dad scoots around the kitchen island towards the door. He opens the door but is bombarded by Jejune.

"Is it true!" Jejune yells towards me. Stunned, my dad freezes holding the door open. "Good luck," he mutters under his breath and heads off to work.

"Is it true!" she asks again with more force, standing between the couches my mom and I are both sitting on.

"Is what true Jejune," I ask exhaustedly.

"Was someone *murdered* today!" she bites through her teeth. My mom leaves and heads for the bathroom. Jejune follows her movement with angered eyes as my mom gingerly closes the door. I motion my arm towards my mom as a sign of an answer. "Those bastards!" she shouts, pacing the living room.

"Would you relax," I shout back. "My mom is really shaken up about it."

"Do you blame her," motioning to the closed bathroom door. "You were there, tell me how they did it."

"They did not do anything," I say, bringing my hands to my head.

"Of course they did. It's Amella's favorite past time to just take people out whenever they feel like it."

"It was a Northerner." I release my head from my fingers to look at Jejune. "Some old man, he was a one."

"Oh well isn't this fantastic!" Jejune throws her hands up. "Now people are getting guns again!" The door to the bathroom opens and my mom returns in her night robe. Jejune ceases her ranting with a heavy exhale and swallowing of her throat. "I'm sorry Mrs. Pharl," Jejune softly states. My mom takes a deep breath in and looks towards Jejune.

"Jejune, would you like me to get some sheets for you?" Surprised by my mom's question, I find the clock in the kitchen that reads 20:37, almost curfew.

"That's not necessary, but thank you, I have to get back to Stevey." My mom nods, says goodnight, and heads to bed. Jejune follows my mom, her bloodshot eye creeping out. My mom closes her door and the bloodshot in Jejune's eye disappears as she stares back at me. "We will discuss tomorrow."

"I have work," I say as she heads for the door with determination.

"I can plan around that," giving me a thumbs up. Jejune pushes the door open from the bottom with her thick boots. Before the door shuts, I can hear the soft shuffle of pebbles as Jejune begins running home.

***

After a restless night of sleep, I autopilot my way through work. The sky is gray as I walk to our set's headquarters. Not listening, I watch as clear raindrops race one another to the bottom of the windowsill. It has not rained in the North for a long time, almost symbolic, as if the sky is crying for the lives lost yesterday. I finally turn my attention back to the director as he concludes his vision.

"… in the heart of the North. Which is why I called all of you in the Sound Department because I've selected you for the job." Others in my Department look around thrilled, especially this one girl who is a three. I guess any news is exciting to her sad little life. "We don't shoot in North Amella for another two days, but in the meantime, I want footage of the North itself. The people, landscape, and so forth. Unfortunately, due to the weather," his pom pom bouncing as he looks towards the window. "We'll have to hold off on exterior shoots." The girl with three spheres shoots her hand up like a little kid trying to give the answer to her teacher before anyone else in class. "Yes," the director sighs, feeling as though he is interrupted.

"I first want to say thank you for selecting us to be a part of the North Amella shoot," she says with too much appreciation. "I may be overstepping my bounds, but why do you need *all* of us from the Sound Department?"

"Thanks for your concern sweetheart," he states condescendingly. "But if you haven't noticed, North Amella is a pretty big establishment so we're gonna need all the bodies we can get." I scratch my nose to conceal the smirk forming across my face. The director clears his throat to cease the awkwardness of the room. "So, today we will plan and spreadsheet. Tomorrow, hopefully the weather clears up, and we will journey to North Amella." The crew begins mulling about in preparation for the new shoot. Walking through the commotion, I approach the pom pom director.

"Director?" I ask as he flips through piles of paperwork.

"What," he says, without even looking up.

"What if you do not want to film in North Amella?" Stunned, the director stops rummaging through his papers and looks at me.

"If you don't want the job, I will give it to someone else."

"Thank you."

"I will assign you to the exterior shoots tomorrow." He goes back to his papers and I turn to find a group. "But," he adds, reverting my attention back to him. "It is less pay." Not looking for a response, I leave the conversation. I catch the girl with three spheres looking at me in disgust. Ignoring her, I join a different group for brainstorming. While she was in the three ballroom, I was fearing for my life in the six ballroom. She can praise Amella all she wants, but I would feel safer being nowhere near North Amella for a while.

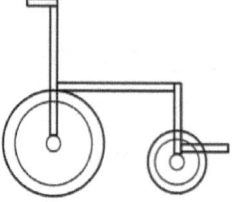

I shake my hand as cold droplets fly off my fingers. On top of walking home in the rain, my hand is killing me from writing spreadsheet notes nonstop for hours. Reaching my front steps, the sound of the key unlocking the door is drowned out by the volume of the rain behind me, like thousands of rats scurrying. The precipitation outside is replaced by the hushed volume of my television.

"Glad to see you let yourself in," I say, closing the door.

"Don't you wanna know how I got in," Jejune asks, guzzling food into her mouth. Her legs are crossed out in front of her, bowl of food in her lap, and her hat is backwards to see the television better. Her scarlet scar radiates against the light of the screen. Like a dog kicking up grass, I scuff my shoes on the rug to help absorb the wetness as I peel my matted jacket off my body. My jeans are glued to my thighs as I run my fingers through my damp hair. "I'll take your silence as a no," Jejune states. I collapse on the couch parallel to her, a yawn releasing from my mouth. "Chip?" Jejune extends the bowl towards me. I finish yawning and tiredly blink my eyes awake. Not wanting any chips from her, Jejune reclines her arm back, letting the bowl settle in her lap again.

"So," Jejune continues, squishing herself into the corner of the couch more. "A person is dead and the North is acting like everything is totally normal."

"Two," I say back.

"Hmm?" Jejune asks, biting down on a chip.

"Two people are dead."

"The more the merrier," she sings, shoveling chips in her mouth.

"Our next shoot is at North Amella." I lean my body over as a sign I want some chips.

"Please tell me you said no," Jejune states, handing over the bowl. I nod and grab a handful of thin potatoes. "Good girl, I raised you well."

The sound of Jejune and I's crunching echoes throughout the house as our conversation goes quiet. As if sensing our silence, the television turns stark white as six chimes fill our ears. Jejune mockingly dances along, the chips mimicking the tune as they swish in the bowl. The white on the screen fizzles out and is replaced with a woman wearing a North Amella uniform.

"Hello Northerners, we apologize for this interruption."

"Who's this chick?" Jejune asks.

"No idea, I have never seen this lady."

"As many of you may know we had a tragic incident occur during the North's beloved Counting Day," she states, her bob blonde hair unmoving, almost robotic like. *"In the six ballroom –"*

"What do you mean you've never seen her, you film all this," Jejune states. Jejune is right, I do film the majority of the North's broadcasting. This was not discussed at the meeting today. The woman is standing in front of light green walls with picture frames which is not our standard backdrop.

"I think this is live," I reply.

"... I am honored to be standing here with one of the brave survivors from this recent event." The camera pans over to the actress from yesterday, smiling and alive.

"I thought you said she was dead?" Jejune exclaims.

"She was." I raise my back off the couch to get a closer look.

"Well she doesn't look dead to me."

"No…" I am at a loss for words but manage to formulate a response. "No, I *swear,* she was dead before she even hit the ground."

"Shhh," Jejune motions, pushing her hand down.

"… thing you would like to say?" I catch the woman on the screen asking. As the actress speaks, the camera zooms out to reveal her sitting in a wheelchair.

"Thank you," the actress says to the camera. "I guess there is not much I can say except I am so grateful that I am alive. My hope is that this event does not shine negatively on the North, but we as Northerners can see this as an opportunity to grow." The actress' six spheres are barely visible as they blend in with the white of her drained face. Her eyes begin to gloss over and the camera cuts back to the woman with the bob haircut.

"What a lovely message. The man that performed this cruel act was shot down by North Amella's well trained crew members. Thank you to those who continue to keep us safe. In light of this event, we remind you all to keep your spheres and do not shed your tears. Goodbye to all and thank you for listening." The blonde on the screen fades as six chimes bring us back to our regularly scheduled program.

"That's all wrong," I softly say. "And that's not even the proper sign off for a video," I state louder.

"I thought you said she was dead," Jejune states again.

"She was!" I stand up snapping my head towards Jejune, confusion and anger in my voice. "I saw her die, the bullet went through her chest," I emphasize, hitting my chest with each word. Jejune raises her eyebrows not saying a word. "She was lifeless," I plead.

"Well good thing Amella took the guy down," Jejune says sarcastically.

"But they didn't," I yell towards her. "He killed himself, I saw him do it." I stop ranting and catch my breath, placing my hands on my hips. Jejune puts the bowl of chips on the couch next to her and slowly makes her way in front of me. She stops inches away from my face, her angered eyes staring into mine.

"So they're lying," Jejune states. My eyes shift back and forth between hers. Jejune remains unblinking, her rebellious scar piercing my perfect six spheres. "They are the ones we are supposed to have the most confidence in and they are lying to us?" Jejune questions. "If they are lying about this, what else are they lying about."

I do not have to respond to let Jejune know I understand. My body collapses back onto the couch as if someone is pushing down on my shoulders, forcing me to sit down and rethink everything that I have been told throughout the entirety of my life. Jejune is right, they're lying. Jejune's anger, her hat, why she hates Amella so much. I am beginning to understand, I just never experienced such a revelation first hand. I *know* I saw the actress die, the bullet went through her chest. No one could survive such an injury, and the old man, he *pulled* that trigger. I think, or maybe Amella *did* kill him. The lights did go out right as he was pulling the trigger...

"Stop that." Jejune snaps her fingers in front of me. I jolt back slightly and look towards her. "You're doubting yourself and that is *exactly* what they want you to do." Jejune sits beside me, my numb body wavering slightly. "You saw the actress die?"

"Yes, but –"

"You saw her die," Jejune snaps back, erasing my doubt. I look directly at her as she lingers for my response. The response she wants to hear, the one she needs to hear.

"Yes," I state.

"You saw the old man pull the trigger?"

"Yes," I exhale.

"And you know that what you saw *is* what you saw." Before I answer, I look directly at Jejune. Her mint eyes and ruby scar are shouting at me to respond.

"Yes."

"Do you see now." Jejune repositions her body to face me. "See, we are too confident in what they are telling us is true, and we are too careless to realize what they are telling us is false." I turn away from her glance, looking to the floor for answers, any explanation other than Jejune's. "Amella is smart. They get us when we're young. Tell us they're going to protect us. Tell us that we can't cry or else we will die to instill fear in us. Tell us that if we don't cry and keep our spheres, they'll keep protecting us from horrors like that," she gestures to the television where the crippled actress appeared moments earlier. "And they tell us to keep our mouths shut about any doubt because if you dare open your mouth, if you dare go against them, they will not protect you anymore."

Still trying to take in this turn of events, I make my way to the kitchen to grab a glass of water. With a million thoughts racing through my head, I devote all my focus on pouring this glass of water. How could I, my parents, everyone, be fooled like this for so long. I bring the glass to my mouth, trying to drown away the shock that is coursing through my body.

"Look at what they have versus what they give us," Jejune continues. "Don't you find it odd that Amella has high tech vein scanners to enter buildings yet we have plain old keys? Or that they have the latest equipment, but we are stuck with broken down televisions and old phones?"

"So, what are we supposed to do about it," I ask, my voice shaky.

"You can't just stop Amella," Jejune laughs. "They're an empire of control." I take another sip of water, gathering my thoughts. "And I know how you're feeling. You want to tell everyone. Try to make them understand, but you can't just go crazy.

You'll be eliminated."

"So what, keep living like everything is fine?" I ask, frustration in my voice. Jejune shrugs her shoulders and nods. "For now," she replies.

"But everything is not fine if they're killing people."

"And they will keep killing people. It's how they keep order I guess," Jejune says, a hint of defeat in her tone. "Knowing them, they are listening to all this." And on that note, the phone rings.

Jejune springs off the couch, her eyes glued to the square on the wall. The sound almost elongates with the anticipation of who is on the other end. Jejune motions her hand towards the phone as if to tell me to answer it. I put the glass down on the counter and rip the phone from its holder to my ear, silencing the ringing.

"Hello?" I swallow and look towards Jejune, shoving her hands in her pockets looking at me for answers. I shake my head with a frown. I prompt to speak into the phone again. "Hello."

"Ya hi sorry I got distracted," the person on the other end says. A sigh of relief fills my body. It is the pom pom director. I give Jejune a thumbs up and she goes back to relaxing on the couch, vanishing into the cushions. Confused on why he is calling me, I resume the conversation.

"How may I –"

"Ya hi Rose right? The sound girl with six spheres?"

"Yes."

"Ya looks like you're on crew for the North Amella shoot."

"I know," I reply confused. "I asked to do exter –"

"No honey, I mean *in* North Amella. You'll be taking Lisa's spot, the three. Amella is holding a mandatory retraining this week for people that were in the six ballroom and lost spheres. Lisa happened to be one of those and Amella doesn't want that kind of negative publicity, you get me?" he quickly tells me.

"Um, yes. I get you." *That girl was a six like me?*

"So I will see you tomorrow."

"Tomorrow?"

"Change of plans, we're meeting at the station by HQ at eight tomorrow."

"What about the exterior –"

"Forget about those shots," he hysterically shouts. "Someone else will take your slot. Okay?" I look across the room to my friend disguised by the couch for support. Jejune and I may not be able to take down an entire empire, but we could start the crumble.

"Okay, I mean yes. Yes, thank you for letting me know. I will see you at North Amella." Jejune's head pops up from behind the couch like a groundhog coming out of its hole. I place the phone back as I hear Jejune roll off the couch and run into the kitchen.

"Did I hear you correctly?" She skids around the island to get to me. "North Amella? Tomorrow? Yes, this is our in!" She begins to reverse direction towards the front door. "I gotta get Stevey, but we will talk. We will talk!" She points at me as she stammers out the door.

"Wait Jejune," I say from the kitchen but it is too late. I do not know if Amella is lying, that actress could have survived, but I doubt it. In any event, I want answers, and I think North Amella has got them.

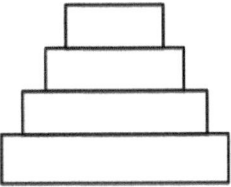

"We need more angles than straight on," pom pom director says. As a yawn escapes my mouth, other members of the shoot sluggishly begin setting up equipment. Upon entering North Amella, it is not as spectacular as Counting Day, not to mention the diminishment of security. Pom pom director continues to circle around the empty lobby, hoping for inspiration to strike. Unlike Counting Day, the lobby is eerily serene. The creamy marble walls reflect my image as if I am hazily moving under water setting up my boom.

As I continue to crane my boom pole around, pom pom director continues to crane his neck around the open area. His gaze stops as his eyes look above him. He snaps and points up to the second floor.

"There," he exclaims. "Can we get up there for an aerial shot?"

"Whatever will help your artistic vision," a voice echoes from a neighboring hallway. I flick my eyes up and, to no surprise, it is the actress, but this one has black hair and is slightly curvier than the stereotypical actress on the screens of the North. My mind flashes to the image of the dead actress on stage. I blink hard, forcing myself back to reality.

"Great because I wasn't gonna take no for an answer sweetheart," pom pom director winks, looking her up and down. The actress politely smiles and steps sideways to reveal crew members rolling in more equipment. "Just when I thought we couldn't get more advanced." Pom pom director places his hands on his hips. "How much of this stuff does Amella have anyways?" he inquires.

"As much that is needed for the shoot," she softly replies.

"Right," pom pom director smirks. "So," he says with an accompanying clap that vibrates throughout the lobby. "I want Amella's equipment in the center of the lobby."

"This is the new Sphere Refiller," the actress states, gently touching the edge of the device. "Amella would prefer to focus on the Refiller for this video."

"Anything for you doll face," pom pom director winks, stepping a little too close to her. The crew members behind her step forward reminding everyone of their purpose. He steps back. "Messaged received." I peer above me, the second floor balcony looming overhead as I secure my connecting headphones. I need to get up there. If Amella has secrets, that is where they would be.

"To get the best shot of the Refiller we can do wide shots and close up shots. While those are happening, we'll get establishing shots overhead." Pom pom director pauses, looking towards the crew members guarding her. "If that's allowed."

"Of course," the actress replies, ignoring the crew members behind her.

"Alright." Pom pom director turns around to face all of us. He selects his camera crew, lights, and then comes to sound crew.

Please pick me.

"Rose get up there and listen to the sound quality," he demands with a sway of his hand. I nod and make my way up the levitating staircase.

That was too easy.

My steps pound throughout the open lobby, as if they are shrieking with my excitement. The scene below me bounces as I hop up each step, finally resuming to a steady picture once I hit the landing. The lobby looks even grander from the balcony. I take in the layout of the second floor and am met with a ginormous map of the States. It is fascinating to see each State in comparison to the North. I have not studied a map of the States since I was in school. Compared to others, we do not cover much territory.

As the camera crew and lights position equipment, I pretend to adjust the size of my boom, even though I will not be using it. As my head faces down, my eyes shift side to side to see the second floor layout. To my right I see one continuous hallway. I shift my eyes to the opposite hallway to see the same thing; the hallways are mirroring one another.

"You guys all set up there," pom pom director shouts to the balcony. The film crew and I give a thumbs up, and I position myself behind the camera putting headphones on. "Okay, the actress is gonna talk about the new Sphere Refiller for the North. We'll get a close up shot down here. For now, let's do a wide shot, play it back, and see if I like it."

The actress takes her mark next to the new Sphere Refiller. It is similar to a dentist chair, but with two handles that curve to fit under your eyes to zap you with new spheres. The red light emerges from the camera as the actress recites her lines. Not paying attention to the scene, I revert my attention back to the hallways. There are no crew members blocking the area that I can see, but the last thing I want is to get caught sneaking around North Amella. I watch the actress like the rest of the film crew, pretending I am interested; the actress is not the only one who can perform.

"With Amella's new technology, Northerners simply have to sit back and relax when refilling their spheres…"

I tune out from the actress' memorized lines once again, continuing to look at the second floor. I focus my attention back to the oversized map jumping out at me. The map is beautiful and intricate in detail with each State represented through landmarks. Shadows depicting mountains and splashes of color for bodies of water. The State borders are visible with bold territory lines, showing where the North begins and ends, but soon my interest in the map is consumed by confusion. I revert my attention from the North to other States. The Northeast is relatively the same size as the North, along with the East, Southeast, and Northwest. The South however looks to be double the size of the North and the West double that. So how is it that the North has the highest numbers for Counting Day? I mean, sure the North has many sixes, but we could not possibly have as much sixes let alone people as the South or the West. So how are we victorious again and again?

"Cut!" I uncover one ear to listen to pom pom director's thoughts and look back down to the lobby. "Alright, can you hear me up there?" he yells towards the balcony. Nods and scattered yeses flow from our mouths down to the lobby. "It looked and sounded good, but we'll do it again for safety." The other crew members and I reset and wait for the countdown. I place my headphones back on, the actress' voice engulfing my eardrums.

I turn back to the map to count the number of territories in each State. I tune the actress out as I carefully count. I know the North has seven territories. That long strip of land in the West, that has to bring in a high count amount. That long strip of land in the West territory is *double* the size of ours so...

"Cut!" I flinch as my head fills with his sharp voice, ripping my headphones off to ease the pain. "Nice job people, you can go home now."

"Two shots and we're done, should've stayed in bed," one of the camera crew members mumbles as he makes his way back to the lobby. I take one last look at the map of the States. Maybe the North is really just that good.

***

My mom and I set the table for dinner. Our eating schedules rarely match up in our family but when they do, my mother does not pass up on the opportunity to have a "proper family meal" as she puts it. My mom thought it would be nice to have Jejune and Stevey over as well, so they will be joining us tonight. I finish setting down the last two plates when I hear Stevey's laughter out in the street.

"Welcome Jejune," my mom says, placing the silverware on the table.

"Hello Mrs. Pharl. Thank you for having us. I apologize, Stevey had to bring his backpack to finish up some schoolwork. You wouldn't mind if he finished it while we eat would you?"

"Of course not dear," my mom replies. "Come sit while I grab the food. Rose, could you wake your father for me?" I make my way to my parent's room and let my dad know it is time for dinner. After he slowly arises from his slumber, we all sit at the dinner table and dig into some well deserved food. Conversation is light and interesting with my family and Jejune. We talk about work and the events of Counting Day, but not too much with Stevey around. As the adults finish up their meal, Stevey diligently completes his schoolwork.

"Based on the crayons I can tell you're not doing my homework Stevey," my mom says with a chuckle. "Let me guess, art?"

"History," Stevey firmly states, not looking up from his paper.

"Coloring in history, who would have thought." My parents and Jejune continue with their conversation while I focus on Stevey.

"How goes the coloring," I ask, putting a fork full of food in my mouth.

"Good." Stevey furiously scribbles. "I'm almost done with the East."

"East?" I ask intrigued. "What are you coloring?"

"A map to help memorize the States."

"Very colorful." I wipe my mouth and glance over Stevey's arm to take a look. I continue to watch Stevey color as I take a sip of my drink but stop. Nervously swallowing, I cautiously place my drink back on the table as my eyes stay glued to the Northern territory. The blue flakiness of Stevey's crayon spans vast amount of territory for the North and my mind flashes back to the map I saw earlier today. "Stevey, can I look at your map for a second?"

"It's some of my best work!" Excitedly, he throws the map in my face and I carefully move the map back to get a better focus. Stevey's map in no way matches the map on North Amella's wall. The border lines do not match up. The long territory from the West is missing. There is no shading for mountains. There are no splashes of color for the bodies of water. It is a completely different map.

"You see this is our State, the North," Stevey smacks his finger on the blue area. "We cover a lot of land compared to the other States, or so Miss Rebecca says. And then here," Stevey drags his finger from the blue to the orange color. "Here is the South which doesn't have too much and the West," Stevey continues, my eyes quickly following his tiny finger movements. "The West doesn't have much at all. Which is why we're number one! And neither does the East but I didn't get to finish coloring that part so I will do that now," Stevey quickly stammers, taking the map from my hands and going right back to coloring.

"Excuse me," I say to the table as I head to the bathroom. I close the door behind me, silencing the conversation in the other room. Perplexed, I stand for a long time in the middle of the bathroom.

Am I going crazy?

I slowly exhale and take a seat on the toilet. I rest my elbows on my knees as I run my hands through my hair, trying to scrape the confusion off my head.

I know what I saw, I know what I saw, I know what I saw!

I shoot my hands off my head and cover my face. At least I think I know. I run my hands back through my hair, the skin on my palms bouncing slightly to the heartbeat erupting from my temples. Frustrated, I open the door and rejoin everyone.

Jejune's comment from yesterday replays in my head: *"See, we are too con-fident in what they are telling us is true, and we are too careless to realize what they are telling us is false."* Maybe Jejune was right, maybe we are careless, or maybe I am too careless. Have I really been fooled? Have we all been fooled?

"Thank you for a great meal," Jejune says. "Ready to go little man?"

"I don't want to, I like it here," Stevey whines.

"Pleasure to have you both, let's do this again soon," my mom says. "Rose, would you walk them out." Faking a smile, I nod and follow them both out the door. I bring my hands to my bare arms, rubbing them for warmth. Jejune crosses her arms, swaying back and forth with a stern look on her face.

"Spit it out," she says.

"What?" I question.

"Come on," Jejune chuckles. "If you're going to *fake* going to the bathroom, at least flush the toilet to make it seem like you're *actually* going." I look at Jejune frozen. Man she is good.

"You know me too well," I say, scratching my eyebrow.

"So," Jejune eagerly asks. "It looks like you've seen a ghost or something." Her eyes sporadically try to read what's on my mind. "Come on Rose, tell me."

I shyly look away, pretending to focus on Stevey as he examines pebbles on the ground.

"Stevey's map," I mutter out.

"I mean," Jejune looks towards Stevey bewildered. "It's not the best drawing but it's nothing to be spooked by."

"No not that," I say, snapping my attention back to Jejune's gaze. "Stevey's map, it is not right."

"What do you mean?"

"The States are all wrong. When I was filming earlier, there was a map of the States on the balcony at North Amella. The States on that map don't match the one on

Stevey's." Jejune tilts her head, her scar glowing in the moonlight. "I know I must sound crazy, but I know what I saw and it wasn't Stevey's coloring."

"So, what are you saying, that what Stevey is learning is wrong?"

"Not just wrong but there are more. Jejune there are more places, more States." I can hear my voice growing with excitement. "I thought I was going crazy, but then I thought about what you said about being too careless and just being confident and maybe, for once, your crazy antics are correct."

"Valid statements," Jejune interrupts. "Valid statements."

"Valid statements," I correct myself. "Jejune, I think you are right."

"Not think. I *am* right," Jejune spits out. "We are *all* being lied to. What did you see? What was different?"

"Well, there was this place out West, and the South is much larger than we thought. But the place out West, it is like this whole strip of land that borders everything."

"So let's go."

"What?" I reply, shock filling my voice.

"So let's go see this massive place that borders everything."

"Jejune we can't."

"I'm serious let's go."

"JJ!" Stevey quickly runs over to us, halting our conversation. "There's a man coming this way," Stevey whispers. Jejune and I both look across the way to see a dark figure approaching. "We'll discuss this later," Jejune quickly mumbles.

"Rose!"

I look towards the dark figure calling my name. I instantly recognize the voice as Chard. He begins to slowly jog, joining Jejune and Stevey outside my front door and all four of us stand in silence.

"Oh right," I say, remembering they do not know one another. "Chard this is Jejune my best friend and her little brother Stevey. This is Chard, we work on films together." They both exchange brief hellos and then Chard directs his full attention to me, shutting Jejune and Stevey out.

"Rose where have you been?" Chard asks almost out of breath. "I haven't seen you on set, is everything okay?"

"Yeah," I say confused. "I am good."

"Are you sure, because you can talk to me about stuff."

"I am fine Chard really," I say with a short laugh.

"Don't push me away," he nervously states.

"Trouble in paradise," Jejune sings, making this awkward conversation more awkward. I shoot an unhappy look towards Jejune. "Well that's my cue. Chard," Jejune extends her hand. "Nice to meet you on this fine moonlit night."

"You as well," he replies, returning the handshake.

"Oh, firm grip," she says with a wink.

"Okay! Thank you Jejune. Time to go now," I blurt out, scooting around Chard to escort her towards the street.

"Very nice to meet you Chard, hope to see you again soon," Jejune frantically says as I push her away. I let out an exhale before turning back around.

"Sorry about that, she can be a little much sometimes." Chard and I stand in the spotlight of the moon for quite some time. "Well," I finally say, breaking the silence. "It is getting late so I am going to head back inside."

"Rose, I didn't come here to make things awkward. And I – I apologize if I did, it wasn't my intention." I continue to stare at Chard as he stumbles through his words, his hands shoving deeper into his pockets. "It's just – I wanted to make sure you were okay because you're the only friend I got right now. All my other friends either moved to a different State or lost all their spheres so I never see them anymore. So – I wanted to make sure that you were okay and if you need anyone, anytime, I'm here."

Chard. The handsome, blue eyed bombshell. Who would have thought he was a big softy. Chard keeps his hands in his pockets, nodding his head, as if convincing himself his speech went well.

"Thank you, Chard," I simply say. "I really appreciate you coming here to tell me that."

"No need to thank me," he smirks. "Well, I don't want to hold you up and you're right, it is getting late so I should get back before curfew."

"Curfew, you still got lots of time," I say with a laugh, trying to lighten the mood.

"Oh no I live on the other side of the North," he replies, gesturing behind him. "So I got a long way home, but I'm glad you're doing okay. Have a great night Rose." Chard swiftly turns around and starts his way home, the scuffing of his shoes slowly fading with each stride. I take one last look at Chard as a small smile rises to my cheeks; chivalry is not dead.

***

"I think we should go now. The sooner the better," Jejune says, shoving a handful of chips into her mouth. To avoid questions from my parents, I meet with Jejune at her place the next day to continue our conversation from the previous night.

"We can't leave Jejune, you know how many crew members will be after us," I say, gesturing out towards the North.

"Why do you have to always be so damn logical about things." Jejune continues to jam chips into her mouth, her crunching filling the room. "Can't a girl dream," she pleads, almost spitting chips on me. When it comes to mine and Jejune's way of thinking, her expectations are unrealistic… all the time. Jejune collapses on the couch next to me, throwing her head back in agony. "I wish I could just snap my fingers and be at this mysterious piece of land you saw." I continue to listen to Jejune's munching of chips as I think about the situation.

"I mean," I nonchalantly say. "It would be nice to see what it is."

"That's what I'm saying!" Jejune yells, acting like I am not within earshot of her words.

"I know you will not shut up about it!" I yell back at her.

"Because we can do it!"

"How?" I turn to look her dead in the eyes. She stares back at me, swallowing her chips with no answer. "That is what I thought."

"I was chewing you didn't even give me a chance to say my idea!"

"Oh, now you have an idea," I spit back. "Is it a logical one? No, I am going to guess it is not."

"Jeez Rose." Jejune puts the chip bag on the table. "I did have a good idea, a *logical* idea, but you don't deserve to hear it." Not acknowledging each other's presence, we both sit in silence.

"I know you want to tell me so tell me," I say with an eye roll.

"Nah not really," she snaps back.

"Fine." I put my hands up in defense. "Bet it was not even that great."

"So here is what I'm thinking," Jejune starts. I shake my head with a smirk while she continues her rant. "Based on the map that you saw, I gauge that it would take us a little under a few weeks on foot. Now I know what you're thinking, how do we escape the North and not get caught." I nod my head trying to follow along. "I know you are a good girl and have saved up many vacation points, am I wrong?"

"No, you are not wrong."

"I'm usually not, but anyways, you can use up your vacation days," Jejune says with air quotes, "and some travel time to get away," air quotes again, "and no one will suspect anything."

"What about my parents? They will be suspicious if I am gone for weeks."

"You're very smart. Tell them it is for some grand Amella filming shoot across the States or something."

"Possibly," I say with little confidence. "But what about you and Stevey? Won't it be obvious if we are traveling together and we are just gone?"

"I guess, but maybe Stevey is learning about filming! Or we are also going on a vacation," air quotes again.

"I don't know, Amella is too smart."

"No they are not," Jejune scoffs. "You give them too much credit. If they were really watching over us twenty four seven, and I mean *really*, we wouldn't even be having this conversation."

"Jejune, I mean I could probably pull this off but…"

"What?" Jejune ponders in confusion.

"Your points. I have tons of vacation points because, I am a six but…" I stop. Discussing our sphere difference always makes me uncomfortable.

"I know." Jejune bows her head in discouragement. "I don't have as many points as you to travel that far." I stare at Jejune's scar but revert my eyes when she pops her head back up. "I have a plan for that, but I don't think you're gonna like it."

"Jejune, you do know you will be shot on site for doing something like that."

"Not true," she states, trying to defend her idea. "I just can't get caught."

"And how are you going to pull that off?" Jejune lowers her head, raising her eyebrows at me with a smirk. "Absolutely not," I reply. Jejune raises her eyebrows higher, almost disappearing under her hat. "No way," I shout.

"Come on Rose," Jejune moans, tossing her head back in disappointment. "Live a little."

"Live a little. Live a little," I repeat with more emphasis. "I will not be living at all, I will be dead."

"No you won't. We just have to do it at the right location and time."

"What if it is at the wrong location and the wrong time."

"Then," Jejune ponders, her eyes quickly searching for an answer. "You just can't think like that," she exclaims, waving her hands around.

"Alright Jejune, I think your JJ hat is on way too tight," I scoff, heading towards the door.

"Where are you going?" Jejune says, following my path.

"I got to go home and regroup from this absurd fantasy you have planned out." Before Jejune can get her last comment in, I swing the door open to a crowd of people forming on the street. Jejune and I exchange a glance before sheepishly stepping out towards the crowd.

The crowd's attention is drawn to something in the middle of the street but my view is blocked. As we approach, people are exchanging hushed mumbles, but many are turning away in deep disgust. Reaching the huddle of bystanders, people's whispers are muffled by the sound of crying. I poke my head over the crowd to get a better view. A young boy's body bounces with each sob as he looks down at the ground. My eyes widen when I realize that this is not just some random young boy. It is Stevey.

Before I can even attempt to stop Jejune, she bolts to the middle of the street like a cheetah. Jejune claws her way through the crowd, not stopping for anything. She grinds to a halt in front of him, her body trembling with disbelief as she lunges down to his level. Frantic, Jejune tries to speak.

"I'm here I'm here. JJ is here. Baby what's wrong. Baby talk to me." Stevey continues to look down, his convulsions becoming more powerful with each tear. "No matter the time, no matter the day, I will always have my big sister JJ. I'm here baby what's wrong?"

"But – but," Stevey says in between sniffles and big gulps of air. "But – you weren't here." Jejune's face sinks like a train struck her entire body.

"I –" Jejune stops, closing her eyes and gaining her composure. "I am *so* sorry baby. I am *so* sorry I wasn't here for you when I promised I would be." I can hear the trembling of Jejune's voice. "But it will never, *never*, happen again. Just please tell me what's wrong." Stevey slowly turns his head to look at the crowd that has formed. Jejune follows his gaze, her head twitching like a squirrel smelling for acorns. "Do you like the show!" Jejune screams towards the crowd. People jump back in utter shock. "A young boy is crying and all you people can do is stand around?" Jejune's words settle in the air, everyone stunned into silence. "Dammit is that all you people care about? Your stupid spheres! Go! Report me! I don't give a shit!"

I look around at the impact Jejune's words have on the crowd. A majority of the crowd begins to walk away, going on with their day but a handful linger, as if pitying the situation. I look at the ones who have stayed as Jejune manages to get any information out of Stevey. Many are blankly staring, many have their heads down, one woman is even... crying! Openly crying in public. I take a closer look and realize that the people who have stayed are threes, twos, and ones; I am the only six left.

My eyes stay glued to the woman with two spheres sobbing just like Stevey, clenching her boney hands to her chest. As if by magic, I watch as her second sphere vanishes from her face as she continues to whimper. Why is she crying? She does not even know who Stevey and Jejune are. Is she really that weak? The woman shakily wipes the tears from her cheeks, and just like that she is down to one sphere.

The quiet crunching of pebbles approaches me as Jejune walks holding Stevey in her arms. His crying has reduced to a soft sniffle as he weakly wraps his arms around her, but Jejune's look of defeat is still predominant. Jejune stops next to me, keeping her gaze in front of her.

"Rose, I don't care what you do." She takes in a deep breath, pushing down her emotions. "But there's gotta be a better place than this, and I'm gonna find it."

***

No one reported Jejune. I guess people were either too scared or too wrapped up in their own lives to waste their energy on such a report. I gave Jejune her space after the incident, spending the next few days replaying the whole thing. Stevey's convulsions. Jejune's screaming. The old woman crying. I found out from Jejune later that a kid in Stevey's class had been bullying him and broke his glasses and that is why he was so upset. I also learned that Jejune was serious about leaving. And, I do not know if it was all the recent events or if I am spending too much time with Jejune, but I was also going to join her in this crazy adventure to find a better place.

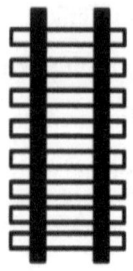

The following days were stressful. I had to take time off of work and convince my mom and dad I was "traveling" for a film. Jejune had to pull a lot of strings to not only get time off from work but take Stevey out of school. My mom asked why Stevey would be absent from school and I told her I did not know, which she believed because Jejune and I have not been talking much. To not draw attention to ourselves, we decided to pack light while we travel. Although Jejune's original plan was to leave at night, I suggested joining the rush of the morning train. Three people boarding the train was not cheap, I had to use my travel points to get us all on the morning commute. Now on the train, Stevey is passed out next to Jejune while her and I discuss our plan in hushed whispers.

"Don't tell Stevey but I have his map. He thinks it is still hanging on the fridge," she states. "He'll *freak* if he knows I have it, let alone have creased it."

"But that map is wrong."

"Yeah, but it's something. We can't be traveling blindly, we'd be crazy."

"Jejune," I whisper. "We already are crazy for doing this in the first place."

"You only live once my friend." She rummages through her bag and finally pulls out Stevey's map. "We're probably going to need allies along the way. I know a few buddies from work but not too many, and when Counting Day happens and we aren't there, Amella will know something is up. So we gotta make it out of Northern territory by then." Jejune unfolds the map for us both to look at. "I'm no expert but it looks like it will take us maybe two or three days to get out of the North. The West," she says, dragging her finger to that area, "is going to be the toughest part because neither of us have been there so we don't know the lay of the land." Jejune folds up the map and shoves it back in her bag.

"You make it seem so easy," I chuckle.

"Well if we plan it out right then yes it will be easy." Jejune takes a sip of her water. "This train goes all the way to the edge of the North. We should just stay on the train until they kick us off. I know of some hotels that we could sleep in for a night, but over time hotels will get pricey and look suspicious, so we'll need allies." Jejune takes another sip of her water. "Hey what about that boy from the other night," she asks twisting the cap back on her bottle. "Chad? Chase? Maybe we can meet up with him."

To be honest I have not thought about Chard once since he came by to do a wellness check. He did mention he lived on the other side of the North, but I have no idea where. Now that I think about it, I should have told him I was leaving, I do not need him showing up at –

"Yo," Jejune slaps the side of my thigh. "You good?"

"Sorry I was just thinking. I will talk to Chard."

"Great. I don't know about you, but we got a long journey ahead of us so time to snooze."

***

Jejune was right, staying on the train was the best plan for now. If this plan was really going to work, we would have to get out of the North as soon as we could. We only have twenty one days until the next Counting Day. Twenty one days until Amella starts coming for us. Twenty one days to find this better place. I hope there really is a better place or we are risking our lives for nothing.

After traveling for a little over four hours, the train screeches to its final stop. Surprisingly, Stevey slept the entire train ride and is not too keen on waking up. As our legs adjust to moving again, we grab our bags and make our way off the train.

Exiting the train, I step into a western part of the North I have never been to before. It seems unreal, but we are actually going to try to find this place.

***

After our long train ride, we camped out at a small hotel and laid low for a couple days. Jejune and I mostly caught up on sleep while Stevey watched cartoons and found ways to occupy himself in the tiny room. I did all the food shopping so Jejune could stay in the room and watch over Stevey. I knew the real reason she did not want to go out was because we were in a new part of the North. With Jejune's scar and unique look, she did not want to draw attention our way and I did not argue. I do not want to be watched in a place I am not familiar with. So we are like hermit crabs staying within their shells. No one bothers us and we do not bother them. While laying low, we mapped our route and planned out our spending of points. I have more points than Stevey and Jejune combined, so we know in time it will become an issue.

"I can always pick up work around here," Jejune says, staring at our map laid out on the floor. "I know people that run boats in this part of town." I nod in agreement. As much as I do not want Jejune to be out in these parts working, I also do not want to use all of my points. As if she can read my mind she continues. "We can only live off your points for so long and, more importantly, Amella will think something is up if you keep spending your points out of our area." The more we talk about it the more fearful I get about the situation. I mean we are only four hours from home, if anything I could just hop on the next train and head back. I hear Jejune repeat herself as I am lost in thought.

"Sorry what?" I reply, coming back to the reality of the small room.

"I said, I think we should stay here for a day or two more. We don't have a plan about how we're going to get there."

"Don't have a plan? Jejune look at the map," I say, gesturing to the piece of paper on the floor under us. Being held hostage in this room, Jejune has been coloring different routes to the unknown piece of land bordering the West. Routes traveling straight through the West, routes going down South and then back up, routes that are long, routes that are short. It is like freshly cooked colorful spaghetti thrown all over the map.

"Yeah but that's nothing," she disregards. "None of these routes take weather change, transportation, or Amella's potential road blocks into consideration. I don't know these territories. One could work, none could work, we could have to back track. I don't know Rose. I need more time." I can tell Jejune is stressing out. So Stevey does not see, she quietly folds the map back up and hides it in her bag. Before I can answer, Jejune brushes by me and sits next to Stevey on the floor.

"I am going to hit the store. Someone likes to eat their chips," my tone geared towards Jejune. Not wanting to stress her anymore, I leave her be with Stevey.

I return back with two bags of groceries, one just full of chips for Jejune. I close the door with my foot as I topple the bags onto the bed next to me.

"Welcome back," Jejune whispers over her shoulder. I look towards her and realize Stevey is sound asleep in her lap. "The little guy is pooped."

I silently make my way to the bathroom when a knock on the door stops me. Jejune cranes her neck trying to make eye contact with me, and we both stare at one another and look to the door. The knocking repeats. Jejune raises her eyebrows at me.

"Who is it?" she whispers. I give her a shrug as my heart begins pounding. The knocking happens again, this time with more force. "Answer it." Heading to the door, I cautiously tiptoe. Before turning the handle, I look back at Jejune for reassurance. "Today would be nice," she hisses. I turn back to the door, my eyes glued to the chipping wood. I turn the handle and crack the door open, revealing half of my face to our visitor.

"I gotta say, you look strikingly different with just three spheres."

"Chard?" I swing the door all the way open. A mixture of relief and wonder trickle down my body.

"There you go," he gestures to my face cheerfully. "Six spheres, that's much better," he says with a smile.

"What are you –" I stop and peer over to Jejune. Her neck is like a giraffe as she tries to see who is at the door. I step outside and shut the door behind me. "What are you doing here?"

"I am visiting my brother who lives five minutes from here and decided today would be a good day to go shopping. While there I noticed a girl with short brown hair and six spheres and thought to myself hey, I know a girl that looks like that, her name is Rose." Chard flashes a smile as he tries to hold in a laugh. "And then," he continues as a laugh escapes through his teeth. "And then I thought, why would Rose be on this side of the North?" Chard stops his monologue looking for an answer. I stare at him in silence as he raises his shoulders to his ears. "So I had some time on my hands and decided to see what you were up to and found out you were staying here."

"So… you have been following me?"

"When you say it like that, it sounds really creepy." He tilts his head up, a tiny smirk on his face. "So, why are you on this side of the North, if you don't mind me asking?" I quickly think about my answer. I cannot tell him the truth, but how else can I explain why we are here? I wish Jejune had answered the door, she can lie no problem. I open my mouth and am about to spit out a fib when a little drizzle of rain begins to creep upon us. Within seconds the little drizzle erupts into gallons of rainfall. I open the door behind me and Chard follows, slamming the door shut, unaware of Stevey sleeping.

"Jeez Rose way to be quiet," Jejune screams. Her face relaxes as she sees that there is a second body in the room. "Oh, excuse me." Stevey remains in Jejune's lap, rubbing his eyes with his tiny fingers.

"Jejune you remember Chard," I say, presenting him next to me.

"Hello," he quickly waves. "I apologize for waking you up."

"No need," she replies.

"I don't want to impose on your time. Rose," Chard lowers his voice as Jejune moves Stevey to the bed. "Maybe we could catch up, just the two of us. We could get dinner or something, on me."

"Dinner sounds great," Jejune interrupts. I guess Chard was not speaking soft enough. "This one wants more than just cheap snacks from the store," she jokes, referring to Stevey.

"Um, that would be great," Chard replies.

"How about tonight?" Jejune asks, approaching Chard and I. I give Jejune a look to make her shut up but she is not getting the hint.

"I mean," Chard questions. "If you don't have any plans then –"

"Nope, no plans," Jejune says, hitching her shoulders up. "So tonight then?" Jejune surveys back and forth between myself and Chard.

"Tonight sounds great," Chard states back.

"Then it's decided. Come back in a few, us gals gotta get ready." Jejune escorts him to the door.

"Okay, see you guys later I guess." Jejune opens the door, the rain echoing through the room. Chard gives me one final look with a two finger salute, slouches forward, and steps into the storm. Jejune shuts the door the second he leaves. My forehead begins to wrinkle as my eyebrows form aggravation.

"Jejune what was that?" I ask sternly.

"I just got us free dinner is what that was." She flops on the bed placing her hands behind her head, satisfied with herself.

"I thought you wanted to keep a low profile?"

"He seems harmless," Jejune shrugs. "Besides, he did come all the way here to check up on you. I guess our profile isn't that low if he already knows where our hide out spot is."

"You are something else," I say, finally heading to the bathroom.

"Don't take too long we got a dinner tonight," she yells at me through the closed bathroom door.

***

As instructed, Chard came back to the hotel later to meet us for dinner. The rain had cleared up and left a musty feel in the night air. The restaurant is a small sit down not too many blocks away. Upon entering, it is blatantly obvious Jejune and I are under dressed. We are both in plain shirts and jeans whereas Chard and Stevey are both dressed to impress. Stevey wanted to look sharp for dinner so he picked out a button up shirt and slicked back his hair. I wish Chard would have informed us of a potential dress code.

With all the traveling Jejune, Stevey, and I have done, we have weight to spare. After weighing ourselves and being escorted to our table, for once, we can all indulge without worry about reaching our maximum limit. Waiting for our food, I wipe the condensation off my ice cold glass.

"Chard, please do tell me about yourself," Jejune asks, placing Stevey's napkin over his lap.

"Well, as you know, I'm friends with Rose and we both work in the Film Industry. I work for the Light Department. Without me, you wouldn't see anything we film." Jejune sneaks a laugh.

"Funny this one," she says, directed towards me.

"Of course, everyone has to have a sense of humor," he replies.

"Cheers to that," Jejune says, raising her glass to the middle of the table. Stevey follows suit, feebly holding his drink up with both hands, a smile plastered on his face. Chard flashes an uncomfortable smile my way, also taking a sip of his drink. I observe the restaurant as I see people staring at our table, more specifically Jejune. Safe to say this part of the North has never seen anyone with a scar for a sphere. Jejune assists Stevey in placing his drink safely back on the table and continues talking. "You know it's okay to stare I don't mind," Jejune says, looking straight at Chard.

"Um," Chard clears his throat, shattering his silence. "I'm sorry I haven't met anyone that is missing a sphere like that." Chard points to Jejune's face but quickly retracts his hand back to his lap.

"It's okay," Jejune laughs. "Trust me, I wish I had your perfect six sphere face, but things are different for me." She scopes the restaurant. Spectators look away acting like they were not also staring.

"People always stare at JJ," Stevey loudly whispers across the table.

"I don't blame them, it's a cool scar," Chard whispers back. "Makes her look badass."

"Yeah, makes her look badass!" Stevey repeats.

"Language little man," Jejune snaps back. "But thank you. Although I'm sitting across from a couple of sixes, I don't feel less worthy." Chard fumbles for a statement back. "I'm kidding!" Jejune exclaims with a laugh. "Gosh Chard, I thought you had a sense of humor."

"If you ever want it fixed," Chard says. "My brother is an expert in refilling spheres." Before I can intervene, our food is briskly placed in front of us. We all begin to eat except for Jejune.

"Thank you for the offer, but unfortunately, this scar is permanent," Jejune says, getting her utensils ready to eat.

"Oh no, he is the best of the best, a true miracle worker."

"Really?" Jejune asks in curiosity.

"Yup," Chard continues, swallowing his food. "He works at SRC, the Sphere Refill Center. You know, the people that add spheres to your face, about ten minutes from here in the Northwest."

"The Northwest?" Jejune asks.

"I did not know you had a brother," I say, cutting into my food.

"A brother with a very prestigious job," Jejune adds staring at me. "In the

Northwest you said?" Jejune asks again.

"Yup, two years older than me. In fact," Chard continues, "my brother and I are in a bet right now to see who can save up the most points. We are planning on taking a month off of work to travel together."

"Like we're doing right now!" Stevey chimes in with excitement.

"Exactly," he replies with a big smile towards Stevey. "Anyways, I know my brother is crazy busy with refill orders, but I'm sure he can squeeze you in."

"You would do that?" Jejune asks.

"Yeah, why wouldn't I?"

"I don't know," Jejune twitches her mouth searching for an explanation. "I don't have much faith in other people," she confesses shaking her head.

"To me," Chard states. "Good people should help good people."

"Well thank you. I would really appreciate that," she says with a smile. We continue to scoff down our food. I carefully twirl my spaghetti around and around my fork, entranced as the loose noodles connect together. I become distracted as Jejune incessantly taps her knife on the table. She finally stops. "Could we have an appointment tomorrow?" she blurts out.

"Jejune." I halt my spaghetti twirling. "I think that is a little forward." She raises her eyebrows at me as if she is telling me to shut up with her eyes.

"Um," Chard dabs his mouth with his napkin. "I mean –"

"You know what," Jejune interrupts, holding her hands in the air. "I'm sorry. I got overexcited." Jejune looks to Stevey, delicately brushing his hair back. "When you were talking about your brother, I thought about Stevey and how much I know he wants me to have my six spheres back. Having less points, it's hard to feed two mouths. It would mean a lot to us." Jejune trickles her hand off Stevey's shoulder while her words hover over everyone.

"I'll give him a call right now," Chard replies, pushing his chair back. "I saw a point phone out front."

"What, no, Chard we are eating," I say, putting my hand on his shoulder.

"It will only take a second," he shifts his body, making my gesture irrelevant to his decision. Stunned, I turn to Jejune who is shoving food down her throat. She waves her fork at me as she works on grinding down her food to swallow.

"That's a good dude right there," she remarks.

"Jejune, I thought," I stop and glance at Stevey attempting to cut his food. Instinctively, Jejune covers his ears and nods for me to continue. "I thought you said the damage to your sphere was irreplaceable."

"Oh yes it can never be fixed," she chuckles, uncovering Stevey's ears. "But this is good because it works out in our favor."

"What? What are you talking about?"

"Trust me. All I need you to do is take that hot piece of ass out for a walk tonight."

"Hey JJ you said ass," Stevey chuckles through a huge grin.

"Yes I did, don't repeat that word," she says in a half serious way, ruffling his hair. Nervous, Stevey dips his fingers in his water, slicking his hair back again.

"Who Chard? Why?" I ask genuinely confused.

"After we finish ask him to take a nice, long walk around the neighborhood. Show you around."

"What will that accomplish?" I continue to pry.

"A lot," she sternly replies.

"How am I supposed to do that," I say quickly, as I can see Chard coming back to the table.

"Just ask, and when you see me on your walk, *don't* react, and make sure you get him near a vein scanner," Jejune quickly mutters, going straight back to eating her food.

"Didn't answer, but I left him a voicemail," Chard joyfully states as he pulls out his chair. "Waiter," he flags down before settling back into the table. "Another drink please."

"Of course sir," the waiter replies and walks away.

"I can't thank you enough," Jejune says with the utter most sincerity.

"No need to thank me," Chard smiles, resuming his meal consumption.

"My apologies sir," the waiter states returning back to the table. "Your request has been denied as you have reached your weight limit for the evening." The waiter nods and leaves the table.

"Damn," Chard states with defeat. "Amella gets me every time." Stevey arches his back letting a huge yawn escape his petite mouth.

"Well, I'm gonna take this little guy back to get some shut eye." Jejune flashes a glance my way as she begins to wrap things up. Following her orders, I swallow a golf ball size of courage.

"Chard, do you want to go for a walk? Show me around the neighborhood?"

"Yeah totally," he replies, turning his attention to me. "I'll be the best tour guide ever."

"Well, you two have fun. Chard," Jejune extends her hand. "Pleasure having dinner with you." He firmly grasps and shakes Jejune's hand. "Rose, I'll see you later tonight at the hotel," she concludes, following with a quick wink.

"Goodbye!" Stevey shouts, rounding the table to give Chard a tiny sized hug. "It was nice to meet you."

"Oh," Chard reacts surprised. "Thanks Stevey. It was nice to meet you too," he smiles, hugging him back.

"Sorry, he is a hugger," Jejune confesses.

"No need to apologize," Chard smiles as Stevey gives me a hug as well. Jejune nods as her and Stevey leave and she gives me a final eyebrow raise.

"So," Chard says, looking at just myself left at the table. "Where would you like to go?"

"I thought you were going to be the best tour guide ever?" I playfully snap back. "You should already know."

"So you never told me."

"Told you what?" I ask.

"Why you're here," Chard states. "Why are you all the way on *this* side of the North?" That was a great question and a question to which I had not thought of the answer. I ponder valid lies in my mind as we slowly walk the deserted streets of the North. Chard continues to stare at me in the moonlight, awaiting my response.

"What, a girl can't do a little traveling," I remark with a hint of attitude.

"No, nothing wrong with traveling." Chard smirks and fishes inside his leather jacket. After some time, Chard finally finds what he was searching for. He carefully unscrews the top of a silver flask and brings it to his mouth. Chard catches me staring at him and releases the flask from his lips. "Where are my manners," he giggles, presenting the flask to me.

"No thank you." He shrugs and continues to drink. "I did not realize you were such a drinker."

"Not by choice," Chard replies. "I get it from my old man."

As we continue down the street, Chard's drunken state increases as his walking becomes staggered and his words become more slurred. Uncomfortable, I search for anything to focus on other than Chard attempting to walk in a straight line. As if the street could hear my thoughts, I spot a point phone.

"I am going to make a call if you do not mind," I mutter, making my way to the point phone.

"Wait, wait, wait," Chard spits out. He hovers in front of me, holding onto my shoulders for balance. Looking past his shoulder and smelling his stench breath, I spot Jejune creeping up behind him into the point phone. Even though Chard is drunk, I keep my eyes locked with his as to not prompt him to turn around. "Rose," he says. I look into his eyes which are usually warm and comforting, but looking at them tonight, I sense a hint of pain. Flicking my eyes over his shoulder, I watch as Jejune presses her wrist against the phone and pays points to make a call. She brings the phone to her ear and motions for me to get closer.

I make eye contact with Chard again and slowly start walking forward. He begins to stumble backwards, squeezing onto my shoulders for more balance. It suddenly hits me what Jejune's "plan" is.

"Chard," I say timidly. "I am really sorry."

"Sorry? Sorry for what?" he questions with a slight burp.

"Hey!" Jejune yells, catching Chard off guard. He lets go of my shoulders, but before he can fully turn around, he is struck in the head by Jejune with the phone. We both watch him collapse to the ground and Jejune rushes to place the phone back on the receiver. "You were supposed to get him near a vein scanner." She begins dragging him onto the sidewalk. I close my eyes in disbelief; this is her genius plan. She stops, his body sprawled out on the ground as Jejune firmly grips his arm.

"Are you going to help me or not," she says, aggravation in her voice. I open my eyes, swallowing my disappointment.

"This is low, even for you."

"We don't have time to discuss and it's not," she snaps back. "I have gone lower." I walk towards Jejune, grabbing Chard's other arm and hoist him up the cement sidewalk. A wave of disgust washes over me as I watch his unconscious body jerk back and forth. We finally reach a vein scanner and let go of his arms as they flop onto the ground. "Okay you grab under one armpit and I'll grab under the other," she says with exhaustion in her voice.

"I can't believe I'm doing this."

"Just do it," Jejune snaps back. We both bend over and lift him up, letting out a grunt. Hobbling over to the vein scanner, Jejune smacks his naked wrist onto the screen. The screen flashes to reveal Chard's information. Jejune presses on transfer and all of Chard's points are sitting there, waiting to be distributed and taken. Jejune flicks his wrist off the screen, leaving me to hold his body as she continues to press buttons. I catch Jejune hit the select all button.

"You cannot take all of his points," I defend.

"What does it matter, we need them." Jejune continues to drag her finger across the screen.

"They are *his* points, *he* earned them."

"Well, now *he* will learn not to get *too* close to people." She turns back to the screen and continues clicking buttons. "Or too drunk," she adds. Too tired to argue, I watch as his points are selected. Jejune connects her wrist to the scanner, accepting all of his points, and instantly the transfer is complete. "Alright let's go," she says turning to me.

"What," I say, looking at her bewildered. "We are just going to leave him here in the middle of the sidewalk? It is almost curfew, he will be killed if he is lying here when night crew come!"

"Rose, we don't have time." Jejune looks at me with Chard's rag doll like body in my arms. "Stevey is alone in the hotel room, I don't want him to wake up."

"Yes! Yes we do have time! It is the least we can do. The least we can do is make sure he does not get killed tonight." Jejune does not move. "We are taking him back to the hotel."

"The hotel!" she screams. "You cannot be serious."

"Yes I am serious," I shout, adjusting his body. I look up at Jejune, her face almost as red as her scar. "Do you really want blood on your hands?" With that comment, Jejune comes to my aid.

In an ungraceful fashion, we continue to move Chard back towards our hotel. Surprisingly in this part of the North no one is outside. As we continue to lug his body across town, I take more notice of the houses around. Curtains are shut. Lights are out. The place seems empty, like no one is even here. The night is silent except for the occasional grunt from either Jejune or myself in addition to our continued heavy breathing. Although it is not curfew, Jejune and I take pause at every alleyway in the event a night crew member is lurking in the shadows. To be honest though, I do not know what Jejune and I would do if we ran into someone. How do you explain why you are dragging an unconscious man through the streets?

I would be lying if I said I wasn't nervous. The morning spotlight of the sun has been flashing in the sky for hours and Chard has not awoken. Maybe Jejune hit him too hard. Not able to take it anymore, I open the front door and slam it as loud as I can. The noise shocks Chard awake; thank goodness. In his dazed state, I explain that he had too much to drink and tripped face first onto the sidewalk. I let him know Jejune was so excited about getting her scar fixed that her and Stevey left for the SRC. Luckily, he believes my story; Jejune must have knocked him out pretty good.

"Oh man, I totally forgot about that, I gotta call him." Chard struggles to get up and place his wrist on the phone.

"No," I exclaim. "I am sure they are there by now."

"Makes sense," he says, feeling the side of his head, pain scrunching his face.

"I am planning on heading out in a few, but feel free to stay as long as you would like."

"Oh no I gotta go home, shower, and do some shopping. Maybe ice my head and get something for this hangover." He continues to massage his skull.

"I thought you went grocery shopping yesterday?" I ask, beginning to pack up my belongings.

"I was planning to but then I was really caught off guard when I saw you there."

"I forgot, you decided to stalk me instead." Chard laughs, giving his head one final rub.

"Thank you for letting me stay the night," Chard says, heading for the door. "Apologies for drinking too much, I wish I could say this hasn't happened before."

"No worries, I had a fun time. See you at work?"

"See you at work," he responds, giving me his classic two finger salute. Chard leaves and the door shuts. I wait until I can no longer hear his footsteps.

"He is gone," I say into the air.

"Jeez, I thought he would never leave!" Jejune swings the bathroom door open to reveal her and Stevey. "Thanks for letting me stay the night. Of course, I had a fun time," she repeats in a mimicking tone. "Ugh, barf in my mouth."

"Jejune that was a close one. He was going to try to make a phone call with no points. How do you think I was going to explain that if his wrist connected with the phone?"

"Well it didn't, so no need to worry about it." Jejune remains squatting as Stevey jumps like a fish out of water onto her back. "Have you two even made out yet?" Jejune asks, trudging out of the bathroom with the weight of Stevey.

"JJ that's gross," Stevey uncomfortably laughs in her ear.

"No, you're gross." Jejune turns her back towards the bed as she releases Stevey from her grip. Stevey squishes into the bed like a graham cracker suffocating a marshmallow as he erupts in laughter. Jejune turns around to stare at the both of us. "What are we going to do stay here all day, let's move it people."

I do one last check of the bathroom and under the beds before heading out. As promised and with points to spare, I call my parents and lie about working. I say that filming is going great and I will be home soon. Although I feel guilty for lying, I know that if I told them the truth they would never have let me leave. Besides, a little white lie never truly hurt anyone. With my hands on my bags and Jejune's hand in Stevey's, we begin our journey further West.

***

Traveling during the day was a good idea. We mesh with everything around us, but similar to last night, there are not many people flooding the streets. We are walking mostly and packed our own food so we do not have to slow down and find a place. It has been a long day and the sun is setting, a soft glow illuminating the roads.

"We're approaching the Northwest," Jejune says. "The woods are starting to pop up so we must be close. Your friend's brother's Refill Center should be coming up as well." We continue walking as the wind becomes cool stinging my bare skin. "What the…" I look up from my feet to see what Jejune is commenting on. The Refill Center is loaded with crew members. It is obvious there is a situation up ahead. "Let's circle through the woods, see if we can find out what is happening."

Jejune grabs Stevey's hand and we begin tiptoeing into the woods. My shoes crushing the leaves underneath me sound like bombs going off in this serene place. We finally find a clearing a few meters from the Center where we can see what is going on but still be hidden. We quietly wait. The crew members disperse, revealing a handful of refill workers outside the Refill Center. They all look out of sorts as their long, white lab coats wave in the wind.

"Something must be going on in the Refill Center," Jejune whispers.

"JJ what's wrong?" Stevey worriedly asks.

"I don't know baby," Jejune says, holding him closer. Another refill worker runs out and all the others surround him. He is talking but I cannot hear or make out what his lips are saying. "Do you hear that?" Jejune says looking towards me.

Before I can even respond, a car comes racing towards the Refill Center, screeching to a halt before the refill workers. They all back up in a panic except for the one who came running out and approaches the car. The car turns off and a tall man with short brown hair emerges.

"Chard?" I whisper in confusion. He rushes towards the refill worker and they embrace. Chard is furiously talking and the refill worker, who I am assuming is his brother, is trying to calm him down. "What is he saying?" I plead to Jejune.

"I can't tell," Jejune says back. Chard continues to ramble. Although we cannot hear him, we watch his movements. He begins rolling up his sleeve and showing his wrist to his brother who examines it thoroughly.

"You don't think…" I begin to say to Jejune. Our eyes lock and I know she is thinking the same thing as me. Chard has realized that all his points are gone. We continue to watch the scene unfold as Chard walks away and covers his face. His brother quickly turns to the other workers and waves his hand telling them to leave.

Chard's brother runs after him to get him to stop. Chard continues to gesture to his naked wrist. His brother draws his attention to the welt on Chard's forehead, anger painting his face. They stare at one another for some time. Chard starts to speak but his brother's hand swings across his face, making him collapse to the ground. I let out a small gasp as Jejune grabs Stevey and pushes him into her chest, shielding his eyes. Chard's brother bends down, grabs his collar, and lifts him back on his feet. Chard is avoiding his brother's eye contact, defeat on his face. His brother is screaming at him as he obediently nods his head. His brother hastily reaches into his jacket and retrieves the flask Chard was drinking from last night. Chard flinches as his brother throws the flask to the ground. Pulling down the skin under his eyes, his brother looks at his spheres to make sure his tears did not spill over onto his face. He pushes him back, yells at him some more, and brushes past him back towards the Center. Chard stays there, staring at the ground.

"We have to go," Jejune quickly says. "It's only a matter of time before he realizes we had something to do with it." I cannot look away from Chard. The hard punch from his brother surfaces on his face as a light pink mark creeps across his cheek. "Rose, we cannot stay here," Jejune says, turning my attention away from Chard. "It will be curfew in a few hours, we have nowhere to run, and we can't go out there with all those crew members. We still don't know what's going on."

"Well, um," I say, trying to focus on us and not Chard. "What is beyond these woods?" Jejune quickly unzips her bag, unfolding the map.

"Hey JJ that's mine!" Stevey exclaims. Jejune whips the map down and covers Stevey's mouth. We all look out towards the Refill Center. Fear explodes in my body as crew members are curiously looking in our direction.

"Damn it Stevey," Jejune hisses in his ear. "You're gonna get us killed." Three crew members approach the woods, guns raised. Jejune uses her other hand to put the map back in the bag.

"Jejune," I nervously say.

"We have to go." Jejune crouches low to the ground, Stevey following suit. Searching below, I rotate my foot to find a rock underneath. I dig the dirt around the perimeter and it finally becomes loose from the ground. Hurling it across the woods, the sound of twigs breaking echoes a few feet away and I watch as the crew members swivel their guns towards the noise. Quietly, I secure my bag to myself and rush towards Jejune and Stevey.

"I think I bought us some time," I say reaching them. With that comment, Jejune stands up, secures Stevey to her, and runs full speed ahead into the woods. The further we run, the thicker and darker the woods become. Jejune is a couple feet ahead of me as Stevey's body bounces up and down on her side.

"Jejune!" I stagger through heavy breaths. "Jejune I think we can stop." We both stop, heaved over gasping for air. I look around us; nothing but trees for miles. "What are we supposed to do now?" Jejune puts Stevey down, unzipping her bag to grab him some water. "We don't know where we are. It's going to be night soon and we –"

"Rose, I know! Will you shut up!" she snaps towards me. Still bent over with my hands on my knees, I look at Stevey, gulping down water. "The sun is still setting. We'll continue to walk until the moon rises. Then we'll find a place to camp out for the night," Jejune calmly says.

"No, we don't even have supplies."

"You got a better idea?" Jejune stares at me, the bloodshot in her eye looking redder than ever. I stand there with no response. "Thought so." Stevey hands Jejune the water jug back and stretches out her neck, giving him a kiss on the forehead. "Let's go while there is still light."

Our travel through the woods is silent. No one speaks. My body is full of exhaustion and it feels as though we are getting nowhere. The moon is serving as our crappy flashlight, not to mention the temperature is dropping.

"JJ," Stevey says, slowing down his walk. "I'm tired."

"I guess here is a good place as any to stop," Jejune exhales. "We'll rest up and continue in the morning." Silently, I place my bag off my back as I drop to all fours. I firmly dust the ground beneath me, trying to create a nice surface to sleep on. Unzipping my bag, I find my jacket and slip my weakened arms through the polyester sleeves. Still in silence, I flip my bag over and rest my head upon it. "Come, I'll wrap you up," I hear Jejune say as I begin to close my eyes.

"I'm so tired," Stevey groans.

"I know you are baby," Jejune lovingly says. "You should be so proud, you traveled so far."

"Can you sleep with me all night JJ?" Stevey worriedly pleads.

"Of course," Jejune softly replies. "Remember, no matter the time, no matter the day, I'll always have my big sister JJ." I fidget a little, trying to make my neck more comfortable in this uncomfortable situation. If I am this hungry and exhausted, I cannot even imagine how Stevey is feeling. "It will all work out Rose," Jejune whispers towards me. "I promise."

I try to think of a response, but the moment has passed. I squeeze my eyes shut attempting to fall asleep, trying to forget the day, trying to forget escaping the crew members, trying to forget Chard. Simply trying to forget everything.

I am awoken the next morning to the sun shining on my face. Squinting, I fight to open my eyes, lifting my head from my makeshift pillow. I slap my hand on the back of my neck, rubbing out a knot and some dirt off. I look behind me to find Stevey wrapped in the arms of Jejune. Stevey's glasses are crooked from lying on his side and Jejune's hat covers her face, their chests moving up and down in unison with each breath. I turn back around to grab a snack from my bag and find someone standing inches away. Startled, I look towards him. He is very skinny, almost unhealthily. His scrawny arms are hardly holding up the pile of logs he has. His dark brown skin is glowing against the morning sun.

"Hi," I calmly say to him.

He does not move, his frightened wide eyes enlarged through his thick rimmed glasses. Although his hair and expression are a little crazy, he is neatly dressed with a pale blue shirt and freshly pressed khaki pants.

"I do not mean to scare you," I say sitting up.

He takes a small step back, his puffy black hair slightly jiggling. A log from his pile topples to the ground, waking Jejune. Jejune tips her hat to look up.

"Hey, who are you?" she demands, quickly waking up. The man flinches at her raised voice, a few more logs falling out of his hands. "Who is this guy?" Jejune asks me with confusion.

"I don't know," I answer shaking my head.

"Hey!" Jejune yells. The man outright jumps, dropping all his logs to the ground. "What's your name?" The man remains silent, his eyes moving very sporadically. "Can you speak?" Jejune asks. Stevey starts to move, slowly waking up.

"Where you bringing those logs to?" Jejune asks, motioning to them. The man remains frozen continuing to stare at the both of us. "Are you gonna talk?" Jejune continues to asks, standing up.

The man sucks in a deep breath, throwing up his hands in surrender and turning his face away. His hands are trembling. Equally confused, Jejune and I both look at one another. I shrug my shoulders in honest confusion.

"JJ who is that?" Stevey timidly asks.

"I'm trying to find that out." Stepping over Stevey's tiny body, Jejune approaches the man. He tries to turn around but Jejune snatches his torso and stands behind him putting him in a headlock. She slides a blade out of her back pocket and holds it to his throat.

"JJ stop!" Stevey screams.

"Jejune!" I scream right after him. Stevey crawls towards me, holding onto me for dear life. I know Jejune can be tough, but I have never seen her act like this before.

"Don't worry," Jejune says, giving reassuring eyes to Stevey. "I won't hurt him unless I have to." Although the man is much taller than Jejune, his legs are bent from being so frightened, making him smaller. With a knife to his neck, he remains trembling squeezing his eyes shut. "I'm going to ask you again," Jejune snickers in his ear. "Where you bringing those logs to?"

"My–my–my house," the man replies through harsh breaths, keeping his eyes shut as if this is all an unwanted nightmare.

"And where would that be?" The brim of her hat presses deep against his temple. The man tries to catch his breath and slowly opens his eyes. They become wide again as he looks towards Stevey and I for help, as if he is a deer seeing a high speed truck approaching, knowing his life is going to end. A petite whimper escapes the man's mouth.

"Where!" Jejune barks in his ear, pulling the knife closer.

"JJ STOP!" Stevey cries. Jejune flashes her eyes to Stevey whose cheeks are wet with tears. Jejune releases her hold on the man and lunges to Stevey. The man takes a deep breath in and falls to the ground.

"I'm sorry baby I just wanted to protect you." Jejune rips Stevey away from me and into her arms as more tears wiggle down his face. I look down at my jacket, soiled with Stevey's salty tears. "Please stop crying. Please stop crying." Jejune props Stevey's head up, attempting to stop his tears from falling.

"Jejune that was not necessary," I say. Quivering, the man pushes his glasses back up on his face and attempts to recollect his logs.

"I–I–I–," the man stammers, still trying to assemble his logs. "Live a–awhile a–a–a–way."

"See, was that so hard to say," Jejune harshly replies.

"Which way?" I calmly ask, cutting off Jejune's commentary. I shift to all fours and slowly approach the man. Like a trainer trying to carefully place a piece of meat near a tiger's mouth, I reach out to the pile of logs and begin to help. "Which way is your house."

"West," he says, avoiding eye contact with me. I adjust my head, trying to make eye contact. His thick rimmed glasses block most of his face, but do not hide the fact that he has no spheres. He is a zero. I have never been this close to a zero before. I thought his glasses were obscuring the spheres under his eyes, but they were obscuring nothing; there are none to be found.

"Um," I say, trying to get past his odd face with no spheres. "Where is the West?" The man grabs the last of his logs and abruptly stands up.

"This wa–way," he motions with his body and begins to leave. With a pile of logs in my arms on all fours, I snap my head to Jejune. Stevey looks at me defeated, now with only two spheres remaining under his eyes. Jejune wipes the last of Stevey's tears and, in a hurry, starts to pack up. I drop the logs in my hand and follow suit. We stalk him a few paces back as the trees become denser and more confusing. The man must truly know these woods.

The sun has begun to vanish during our walk and hunger is setting in. His stark white socks and sneakers illuminate off his brown skin, providing a source of light for us to follow. After what feels like forever, we are met with a small cabin. The true structure of the cabin is consumed by the greenery growing on it as the dirty cedar wood intertwines with the decaying vines all throughout. The two windows on the front and one on the side are boarded up with rotting wood. The uneven shingles on the roof are concaving along with the skinny, lopsided chimney top. The man turns around, still with wide eyes.

"Make sh–sure to step o–o–over the lee–lee–leaves." He turns back around. I look down and notice a narrow strip of leaves and twigs outlining the perimeter of the cabin. The man takes a giant step over the strip and opens the door and we all follow, eagerly wondering what awaits inside.

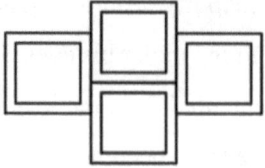

"We–we have guests," the man says, entering the cabin.

In a single file myself, Stevey, and Jejune enter. Contrary to the light outside, the boarded up windows give the cabin a constant nighttime feel. A warm fire to my right is illuminating the contents within the one large room full to the ceiling with crap. Piles of books, papers, boxes, all towering over us are scattered throughout the cabin. Not to mention the walls which are covered with pictures. The pictures create a collage, layered upon one another and masking the wall's true identity completely. People in the pictures are laughing, smiling, posing with one another. Boys, girls, babies… but no spheres on their faces; only skin under their eyes. All of this is unlike anything I have ever seen.

Directly in front of me are worn down green couches separated by a table which is painted with empty beer bottles. An enormous blob of a person is passed out on the couch facing us. The cushions and the crackling of the fire muffle his snores. All he is wearing is a white tank top and checkered red boxer shorts. My eyes look towards the back left corner of the cabin. An extremely neat gray table rests there with a few gadgets and machine looking things in the center. Tools line the wall behind it in an orderly fashion. It is as though a tornado has blown through this cabin but completely missed the back corner.

The man that led us to the cabin quietly places the pile of logs he collected next to the fire. He gestures for us to sit on the open couch and we all reluctantly obey. By pure observation, I gather that the man who led us here, in his neatly pressed clothes, is the owner of the back corner, while the slob in front of us has claimed the

112

rest of this disaster. The man heads to the back corner and pulls on a thin metal string, igniting a single light bulb. He grabs some tools from the wall and begins working completely ignoring our presence. I crane my neck, taking in all the scenery once again. Just like the man who led us here, I stop to take in each photo of the people on the wall with no spheres. How are they so happy without any spheres?

"So, you gonna offer us a drink?" Jejune loudly asks to the man.

The enormous pile of skin lying across from us moves. In a sloth motion, he ungracefully attempts to sit up as burps emit from his mouth. His fat wiggles with each movement, but he manages to sit up and finally look in our direction. Unlike the back of his tank top, the front is covered in yellow and brown stains. His hair is untidy just like the beard wrapping his face, and mirroring the man who led us here and all the smiling people lining the walls, he has no spheres.

"How did ya people get in my house?" the fat man asks with an accent I cannot place. "Did Fred let ya in? FRED! Where are ya?" The fat man unsuccessfully tries to turn around to the man who led us here. Wide eyed, Fred approaches the giant man on the couch. "Fred, did ya let these people in?"

"I–I didn't have a–a choice," Fred says, clenching a few tools in his hands.

"Didn't have a choice." The man looks towards Jejune and myself. "Did ya hurt him?" Fred walks away, going back to his work like nothing happened. "Did ya?" the man demands much louder, leaning forward.

Jejune and I stare at the man frightened to answer and Stevey shyly sits on Jejune's lap. A smile starts to form on the man's face as he lets out a cackle like a hyena. His fat vibrates with each cackle along with the couch.

"Look at ya faces! HA! I really spooked ya didn't I!" The man continues to laugh. Confusion and relief fill my mind as I look towards Jejune who mouths a "what" to me. "Fred! Fred! Did ya see their faces, priceless. I'm just messin' with ya guys. Welcome," the man announces, presenting his arms. "Now did I hear somethin' 'bout gettin' a drink? I'm sorry where are my manners. Ladies… and gentleman," he adds, winking at Stevey. "My name is Frank. What are ya names?"

"Well," Jejune clears her throat. "My name is Jejune, this is my little brother Stevey, and my friend Rose."

"What," Frank says as his eyes become wide. "What are ya names?"

"Jejune, Stevey, and Rose," she repeats.

"Oh." A smile forms across his face, and he opens his mouth but does not say anything, as if he is at a loss for words. He lets out a small laugh and looks to the ceiling shaking his head. "Rose. What a beautiful name," he says, redirecting his attention back to us. "I ain't seen that kinda flower 'round no more though, at least not in these woods. Stevey, I used to know a Stevey once, and Jejune." Frank pauses, scratching his beard in deep thought. "Ya so tall, but that's an original name, just like that scar under ya eye," he states with a wave of his finger. Frank draws his attention to the table full of bottles and begins shaking each beer, hoping for one that is not empty. Jejune and I exchange a glance. I cannot speak for Jejune, but I am too wigged out to say anything.

"Now I know what ya thinkin'," Frank says, still shaking bottles. "What is a fat white guy like me doin' with a skinny black dude like Fred?" He stops shaking bottles and looks directly at all of us. "Honestly, I ain't got an answer." He begins cackling again, filling the entire cabin with his laughter. "But 'nough 'bout me, what are two young girls and a little boy doin' in the middle of the woods?" With great effort, Frank hoists himself off the couch and begins wobbling to the fridge next to Fred's area.

"Well," Jejune begins. "We were planning on leaving but then we ran into Fred and asked him –"

"Ya *asked* Fred a question. The man don't even speak," Frank yells over his shoulder as he digs through the fridge. "He may be the smartest man I know, but he ain't a talker, that's for sure." Jejune looks to me, anger in her eyes.

"We started to gather that," I say, taking over. "We saw he was carrying logs and thought he might be going somewhere so we asked him and he brought us here."

"That was quite a story." Frank closes the fridge clutching three beers. He places a bottle in front of Jejune and myself and cracks his open, plopping back onto the couch. "But that ain't answerin' my question. What are ya three doin' in the middle of the woods?"

"This little guy really wanted to go exploring," Jejune states, rubbing Stevey's head. "He's always been fascinated by nature."

"Would ya cut the bull crap missy." Frank takes a swig from his bottle. "Stevey," Frank pauses, staring at him, his face becoming serious. "Stevey," he repeats and continues. "Ya look like a kid who likes machines. Why don't ya go see Fred, he'll show ya what he is workin' on." Stevey looks up at Jejune.

"Go on," she says. Stevey hops off Jejune's lap and runs over to Fred's work desk. He climbs up the large stool and starts touching the tools. Fred's body language reveals that he does not want Stevey touching his stuff but he lets him.

"Now I know why ya both are really here." Frank glares at us taking a break from his drinking. "But I wanna hear it from ya."

"How do we know that we can trust you?" Jejune snaps back. Jejune and Frank are left in a stare off. Her five spheres and deep scar piercing through his pale eyes and bare skin under them.

"Good girl," Frank smirks with a tip of his bottle before taking another swig. "I'll take a guess at why ya are here, if ya will let me."

"Be my guest," Jejune joyfully replies, cracking the cap from her bottle off the table. She takes a swig and slumps back in the couch, making herself comfortable. I, on the other hand, keep my spine straight, trying to avoid the dirty couch from petting my back.

"As ya can both tell," Frank begins. "I ain't got spheres on my face like they make ya wear, and by they I mean Amella. Ya I know who they are, they are everywhere." He pauses, tipping his head back for the last bit of his beer. "I'm gonna guess that ya guys are from 'round here 'cause ya clothes ain't too dirty and ya ain't lookin' too shook up. I'm gonna guess the North." Jejune and I nod, letting him know his assertions are correct. "Now I'm gonna guess that somethin' happened to ya little brother back there 'cause ya have a fire in ya and I mean quite literally. I mean look at that nasty scar ya got there," he says chuckling. "And ya will protect him, I can tell. So somethin' happened to him that made ya... just... snap," he emphasizes with a snap of his fingers. "Ya ain't wantin' to deal with whateva it is no more. Ya already had ya doubts Jejune, but that was the last straw." He takes in a deep breath, turning his body to face me.

"Now ya," he exclaims with a point of his dirty finger. "Ya ain't in it as much. This one," he says, gesturing to Jejune. "She's feisty, trust me I know that she's feisty, whereas ya ain't. I can tell just by lookin' at ya. May I?" he asks, referencing my unopened beer. He grabs the bottle, cracking it open off the table. He stops his ranting to really look into my eyes. "Have ya always been a six? I mean have ya ever even cried?" He continues to stare at me, allowing me to process the judgments he is making. "Anyways, Jejune, somethin' happened and ya snapped. Rose, ya decided to come along, and along ya route, ya ended up in the woods. Does that sound 'bout right?" Frank remains in his stance, leaned forward, looking at Jejune and I head on. Minus the comments about my spheres, he did a good job guessing why we ended up here.

"Incredible," Jejune says, breaking the silence with a raise of her bottle. I nod in agreement, forcing a smile of appreciation.

"I could just read ya two like a book," Frank humbly replies. "So, what are ya plans now?"

"We're going to escape," Jejune confidently says. Howling like a wolf, Frank flings his head back in laughter.

"Gonna escape," he chuckles. "Oh boy, 'fraid ya was gonna say somethin' like that."

"Do–don't be fooled. A–A–Amella's beautiful app–appearance camofla–flagues the true hor–hor–horrors that exist within," Fred stammers to get out over his shoulder.

"Cheers to that!" Frank raises his glass, drinks from his bottle, and places it back on the table, the glass thudding against the hard wood. "Fred don't talk that much," he whispers towards us leaning in, his alcoholic stench flowing in our direction. "Has some trouble gettin' all of his words out. When he do though, he ain't wrong. Don't be goin' after Amella, ya ain't gonna win."

"Why not," Jejune snaps back.

"'Cause people have tried and it just, it just don't work out," Frank exhales, picking back up his bottle.

"You don't know that though."

"Trust me, I know a thing or –"

"Well we are going to try."

"Are ya even listenin' to a word –"

"Yes we –"

"NO YA AIN'T!" The room falls silent as Frank throws his bottle on the ground, shattering it into a million pieces. Fred and Stevey jump from the sound. Fred reaches under his desk and grabs two pairs of headphones connected to a bulky square device. He presses a few buttons and covers his ears with them and Stevey follows, continuing on with their gadget work. "Ya ain't –" Frank sniffles, taking a deep breath in. "Ya ain't listenin' to me Jejune," he whispers towards the ground. His body begins to shake as he continues to inhale. Jejune recoils back against the couch as concern changes her body language.

Frank snaps his face up, which is now beat red. His cheeks are moist with tears, his brow furrowed with pain. His nose is shiny and his lip begins to tremble.

"Look at ya two," he spits out. "Brainwashed. Ya don't even know what to do." Frank slaps both hands over his eyes and drags them down, wiping away the water from his face. "It ain't ya fault," he defends, blinking rapidly. "It's just how ya were raised." Frank circles his pointer finger around his red face. "This is cryin'. The thing ya told not to do. Jejune, I can tell ya feel somethin'. But ya," he spits at me. "They got ya good. Not even a flinch."

"Ya know there was a time when we were allowed to cry," Frank continues with his monologue. "We were allowed to show our emotions. Didn't make us weak, in fact, I think it made us better. A little thing called sympathy and empathy that we all had. We would cry when someone died. Which ya know is sad, it's natural to do that. We would cry if we fell and hurt ourselves 'cause that's painful to us. Hell, we would cry at stupid things, even happy things." Frank emits a short laugh through his tears. "Like cryin' when ya child was born or ya thought of a happy memory. I miss that time. I really do." Frank brushes a few more tears from his face and makes eye contact with us both again, a small smile forming on his face. "If ya haven't noticed, I don't care much for Amella. I ain't got spheres left, I am *way* over my maximum weight, as they call it. I ain't even livin' in the Northwest technically, I'm in the middle of the woods with little electricity, and guess what, I'm happy." Frank stops, his watery eyes glistening off the fire.

"Ya know, I'm gonna tell ya somethin'. I want to let ya both know, that it's okay to cry after what I tell ya 'cause it ain't a good story. I'm not gonna award ya points for holdin' in ya emotions like Amella does." Jejune and I stare at Frank, numbness over both our faces.

"I knew a guy once, a bright fella, too smart for his own good." Frank stops and shakes his head with a scoff as he begins reminiscing. "He could see through Amella. He could see the truth. The evilness, the deceit, the pointlessness to not showin' ya emotions; he saw it all. He thought he could take down Amella. He had this whole plan and he was so confident in it. The day he was gonna go through with it though, he killed himself." Frank stops as he begins to frown and tears fill his eyes. The pain is written all over his face.

"I knew him and he would *never* kill himself," he states, raising his quivering voice over his sobs. "He wouldn't do that. He knew they were corrupt and he wanted to prove it and they wouldn't let him. *They* killed him." He begins choking over his words. "So when ya say ya wanna escape. When ya say ya," Frank takes a big breath in, his emotions getting the best of him. "When ya say ya wanna take Amella down, it ain't gonna end well. They always want a corpse and ya both will be next, just like him." Frank stops and looks directly at Jejune, a stillness washing over his face before continuing. "Just like ya father, Jejune. Just like ya father." Frank's heavy sobs become louder, his face continuing to distort with sadness. I look towards Jejune, not knowing what to do.

"Jejune," Frank softly says, taking in huge breaths trying to calm down. "I'm so sorry ya have to hear this for the first time comin' from my stupid mouth, but it's better to know the truth than to not know at all."

Absolute disbelief consumes Jejune's face as she shakes her head rapidly. Jejune stammers for a while before she can get complete words out.

"No. No. My father was in –"

"A fishin' accident," Frank states bluntly, finishing her sentence. "Comin' from the other side of town." Jejune's eyes widen.

"He never went to the other side of town," Frank continues. "He never even made it to work that day. When Amella told me he was in an accident I knew they were lyin'. I had a complete breakdown and of course, I was locked up for it, treated like an animal." Frank sniffles and wipes his nose. Jejune continues to search for words. I look at Frank's red face and Jejune's emotional state. I truly do not know how to feel or how I should feel.

"You," Jejune whispers into the warm air. "You knew my father?" Jejune slowly looks up towards Frank. "I don't remember him talking about you."

"Ah, ya was a youngin' back then," Frank says with a wave of his hand. "Come to think of it…" Frank rocks himself forward off the couch and stomps to the wall full of photos. He brushes his sausage like fingers over a few photos then grips one firmly and peels it off the wall. He turns around and hands the photo to Jejune. Jejune timidly takes the small photo in her hands and stares at the image. "Hell," Frank says, as he ungracefully sits back on the couch. "I was much skinnier back then, but that's the only picture I got of me and ya old man."

Jejune's hat obscures my view of her eyes as she continues to stare intensely at the photo, as if she is trying to dissect every little detail. I hope she is not crying.

"I can't even imagine how uncomfortably awful this is for ya," Frank says with complete sincerity. Jejune does not respond, her body frozen in place as she looks at the photo. After what feels like a lifetime, Frank clears his throat to continue to speak. "Jejune I can't even imagine –" he tries to repeat but is cut off.

"Don't make a difference," she snickers through her teeth. "We're still going to try." There is defiance in her voice. Her trance from the photo is broken and she looks towards me, but her eyes have changed. Her scar seems even larger and deeper in color, the bloodshot in her eye glowing from the fireplace. Frank looks down and exhales.

"I respect ya wishes." He looks up as a smirk forms on his face. "Stubborn just like him." Jejune remains silent as Frank clears his throat. "Fred and I will get ya on route to the border tomorrow. Ya can borrow one of the boats we have. We ain't usually goin' to the West but," Frank stops, the redness and pain in his face creeping back up. "Ya father was a good man, and he would want ya to try, so I will do anythin' I can to help."

"He was a great man," Jejune says. Jejune takes one last look at the photo and reaches across the beer bottles on the table to give it to Frank.

"Keep it," Frank insists. "He would want ya to have it." Frank clears his throat and brushes a tear from his eye. "Fred and I will take the couches tonight. Believe it or not we got 'nother two rooms hidin' 'round the corner. Nice big comfy beds in both. Ya guys can take one each for the night." Frank gulps down the last of his beer. "Boy, I ain't had a good cry like that in a long time," he says with another loud cackle. "I'm gonna go make the beds and get some clean sheets."

"Frank, you don't have to do that," Jejune says.

"Ain't gonna hear it Jejune," he says, struggling to get up off the couch. "Good people help good people. Besides, my fat ass needs the exercise." After a few attempts, Frank finally stands up, shuffling to the hidden rooms around the corner. The room is now silent besides the incessant crackling of the fire and clanking of metal in the back corner.

"Jejune, I am sorry about your dad," I say.

"No you're not Rose," Jejune scoffs and shakes her head. "You didn't even know him." She sniffles and looks at me with her electric lime eyes. "You think you are but you don't even know the meaning of the word." I stare back at Jejune, trying to figure out her reason for acting like this. "Come to think of it Frank makes a good point, have you ever cried Rose, or have you *always* had six spheres?" Jejune gets up, delicately folds the photo and puts it in her pocket as she makes her way towards Fred and Stevey, leaving me on the couch with a whirl of confusion swirling over me.

No, I have never cried, but why does that matter? Why does it all the sudden matter if I am a six? That has never been a question before. Why is it now?

"Alright," Frank proclaims as he wobbles back into the room, snapping me out of my own thoughts. "Fred and I will prepare dinner. Then after we have food we all gonna get to bed 'cause we got an early mornin' tomorrow." A smile scrunches his fat filled cheeks. "This calls for 'nother beer."

After a surprisingly good night's sleep, we all prepare to head out. It was nice to wake up and see Frank wearing pants. More specifically worn down denim overalls with a red shirt underneath, but nonetheless, he is wearing more than just his underwear. Fred has not changed, still wearing his blue shirt and freshly pressed khakis. Jejune and I restocked our bags with water and food. Jejune took a handful of beers as well; Frank insisted we could not travel without alcohol.

"Are we ready to get this show on the road?" Frank asks. We all nod as we pile into the small living area. Fred is tidying up his corner as we proceed to head out. "Come on now Fred, ya can deal with all that mess later," he yells waving his hand.

Frank squeezes through the narrow hallway out the back door and we all follow. With Jejune's commentary last night, we did not talk much after. To be honest, we were all exhausted from the day's events and once my head hit the pillow, I was out cold. As we walk through the dense woods once again, I know I should feel energized and ready to continue our journey. I just cannot stop thinking about Jejune's comments and what she meant by that.

"We ain't got much further," Frank yells over his shoulder. After a few more minutes, we reach a clearing. The trees are scarcer and I can hear the faint movement of water. A handful of boats are leaning on their sides, secured with tightly knotted ropes around the trunks of nearby trees. "Ya chariot awaits," Frank gestures, erupting with laughter. "It ain't the prettiest but it'll get the job done. Jejune, ya a fishin' girl, come help me put this beauty in the water."

Jejune lets go of Stevey's hand and heads towards the edge of the water with Frank. I approach Stevey and look down to see concern on his face.

"You okay Stevey?" I ask.

"I've never been in a boat. Is it scary?" he asks, looking up to me. He is squinting so much from the sun his eyes are basically closed. I kneel down, allowing his eyes relief from the blaring star in the sky.

"It is not scary at all," I say with a smile. "It is relaxing, you may even fall asleep from the movement of the water."

"I am pretty sleepy." He reaches under his glasses to rub his eyes. I cannot even imagine how exhausted Stevey must be. All this walking and lack of sleep and proper food has taken a toll on me, but for Stevey, this must be a cycle of constant depletion for his petite body. I wish he did not have to be in this situation. No child deserves to be hauled on this unstable quest to find the unknown. The loud swash of the boat hitting the water captures my attention. Frank ungracefully grips the edge of the boat as sweat soaks his face and seeps through his shirt.

"Well come on ya two I ain't gonna hold this forever!" he yells to Stevey and myself. The boat sways from side to side as Jejune begins to settle in. She extends her hand for Stevey, his movements barely making the boat oscillate. He clings to her as he uncomfortably eyes the liquid surrounding him. Finally, I climb into the boat sitting down in front of Jejune and Stevey. "I guess this is really it," Frank says, holding onto the rope to keep the boat secure. "In the bag behind ya is everythin' ya will need for the journey. Drinks, food, rope, life vests, whateva ya think ya need is in there. Even supplies to catch fish."

"We can't thank you both enough for this," Jejune says.

"Before ya all leave ya have to promise me somethin'." We all look up to Frank from the low structure of the boat. There is silence except for the faint swishing of water. "Ya have to promise me that no matter what happens ya will be safe. Now ya are brave but ya young, ya are very young, and I ain't gonna be there to protect ya

124

if somethin' bad happens." He stops again as emotion begins to creep upon his face. "I know we just met ya, but ya guys are good people. There ain't a lot of us left and I ain't lookin' to be goin' extinct. So please, be careful."

"We promise Frank," Jejune smiles, holding Stevey closer. Before Frank begins to release his hold on the rope Fred stammers closer to the boat.

"Here," he says, stretching out his quivering arms. In his hand is a pile of what looks like metal junk. With Jejune holding Stevey, I carefully take the pile and examine each piece closely. "The bl–blue squares are for pow–power. They run on–on so–so–solar ener–ergy. Keep them in th–the sun and the ot–others are ti–tiny fla–flash–lights."

"Fred did you make these?" Jejune excitedly asks, looking at the pile.

"Yes."

"Wow! Cool!" Stevey comments.

"Well I'll be damned, that is the most I've ever heard Freddie talk," Frank exclaims. Jejune and I continue to pick apart the pile as Stevey intriguingly looks, mouth open wide in amazement. Jejune scans through a handful of what look to be indigo toothpicks.

"What are the skinny ones?" she asks, holding the object up for Fred to see.

"Um," he says, pushing up his glasses. "For emer–emergency only." Jejune carefully places the object back into her palm. We both look at one another and then back at Fred. His eyes are sporadically looking at everyone around as we await an explanation.

"Well," Frank hollers, making Fred jump and causing his wild hair to shake. "Ya gonna explain what type of emergency ya mean." Fred swallows and begins to fidget with his shirt, wrinkling the smoothness.

"Poison," he states. Jejune's eyes widen and I immediately let go of the toothpicks I am holding.

"Enough said," she replies, cautiously placing them in her bag. "I think we're all set."

"Ya father would be proud Jejune. He really would," Frank says.

"I'll make him proud," she replies, letting Stevey back in her arms and holding him even tighter. "I promise."

The rope slips through Frank's hand as the boat drifts into the water and Stevey nervously clenches Jejune as he experiences his first boat ride. I look back to Fred standing in his stoic way and Frank standing stern with his arms crossed.

"If ya ever need us, ya know where to find us!" Frank shouts across the water. Frank looks to the sky and starts to speak, but his words are drowned out by the hissing motor pushing us forward. My eyes stay glued to Fred and Frank until my vision is met with a wall of trees, and just like that, they are gone.

***

We slowly speed across the intense teal water. Jejune resembles a phoenix perched at the front of the boat. She is in her element, her confidence within this feeble structure radiating as the morning sun makes its way to the center of the empty sky. Stevey is practicing his spelling in the middle of the boat, his quiet reciting muted from the buzzing motor behind me. After we made it a few miles down the river, Jejune taught me how to steer the motor as she navigates up front. Jejune let me know that this was not going to be a quick boat ride. According to her map and Frank's knowledge of this river, the West would take a few days to get to. If it were not for Jejune, I would be completely lost. I know nothing about boats, nothing about fishing, and nothing about navigating bodies of water. This is in no way my show; it is all her.

The boat becomes unbalanced as Jejune leaps to my side. She reaches for the motor as I lean back and out of her way. The motor fades as the boat comes to a gradual stop. Jejune finishes finagling with the buttons on the motor and directs her attention to me. Although her hat casts a shadow from the nose up, I can sense something behind her eyes. The bloodshot in her eye plays peek a boo as she scans my face.

"You ready?" she asks me, a smirk across her lips.

"For?"

"You, Rose Pharl, are going to learn how to fish."

***

The bobber floats on the surface, rocking with the ripples of the water. It took many tries to cast my line successfully, along with puncturing the slimy bait through the hook. After getting a taste of Jejune's occupation, I will think twice before complaining about holding my sound boom. The air is still, only the faint whispers of leaves from trees fill our ears. Jejune remains in a hammock like position as she keeps her eyes on the lines. With her JJ hat backwards and her hands clasped behind her head, she is so content. After some time, I shatter the calmness, my own guilt ultimately erasing her sense of peace.

"I am sorry about your dad."

"Nothing to be sorry about," she frowns, still entranced with the fishing lines. The light choppiness of the water reflects against Jejune's eyes. "But thank you." She turns her head to look at me. Our faces mirror one another with a smile. Her jade green eyes compliment her butterscotch skin along with the fresh water beneath us. It is rare to see all of Jejune's face.

"Do you miss him?" I ask.

Jejune turns her head back towards the water and slides her hand in her pocket. She flips open the photo from Frank and a delicate smile forms across her lips. She shifts her body towards me and I grab the photo from her hands. Two men are standing with huge smiles and fishing rods in their hands in a white wooden boat. Although much thinner, I can tell the one on the right is Frank and the one with the bright green eyes who looks strikingly like Stevey is Jejune's dad.

"More than you can imagine," Jejune responds. I hand the photo back to her, and she lies back to take in the warmth of the day. The sun is acting like a spotlight on her copper red scar, presenting the uniqueness of colors. Red, garnet, apple, and sangria all intertwined like an old knotted ball of yarn. Such a distraction from the smoothness of her five stark white spheres. After all these years, I am still tempted to always look at her scar and forget all the other features of her face, and after all these years, I am still tempted to ask her about her scar.

"Can I ask you something?" The words escape my mouth without even thinking if it is okay to ask.

"Sure," she says, getting more comfortable. "You know, I wouldn't want to be anywhere else right now. It's so great out here." I rotate my head, taking in the scenery around us, still contemplating if now is the right time to ask. Is now the right time to get the answer to this mystery I have always wondered about? "Anyways, what were you gonna ask?"

I clear my throat, preparing myself to ask this big question. Suddenly, the bobber begins to violently bounce and the reel unravels rapidly. The echoing of hollow wood and sloshing water erupt as Jejune stands up.

"Reel it in! Reel it in!" she instructs. Flabbergasted, I scurry to the edge of the boat and fumble for the handle, and with great force, grind the line back in. In the midst of this, Stevey is awoken and Jejune grabs hold of him. "Stevey! Rose is catching her first fish!" He immediately withdraws from his sleepy state as a huge smile plasters his face.

"Go Rose!" he cheers. I continue to crank the handle as Jejune and Stevey act as my cheerleaders, chanting my name with each full cycle of the handle. The calm water is broken from the aggressive movement of the fish flying through the air. I stop cranking the handle as shock scurries through my body. Stevey jumps with joy as Jejune reaches past the boat to grab the silver fish.

"Rose you caught a fish!" Stevey squeals.

"A good sized one too. Beginner's luck," Jejune says, keeping the fish's mouth open.

"I caught a fish," I repeat in amazement. The sun displays the concrete gray and broccoli green scales of the fish as it begs to breathe. Jejune cautiously slides a pair of pliers into the gills of the fish. Stevey stops cheering and covers his eyes as Jejune meticulously fidgets to safely free the fish as it struggles.

"Don't worry Stevey, I'm doing this so it won't be in anymore pain." Jejune drops the pliers and reaches in its mouth for the hook. "See, all done." Jejune holds the fish on both her palms, as if presenting a gift to Stevey. He slowly removes his hands from his face and opens his eyes. "Go ahead," Jejune encourages. Stevey sticks his arm out. He brushes the fish then retracts his hand.

"Ew that is slimy!" He shakes his hand, trying to rid his fingers of the texture. Jejune and I laugh, and she places the fish down, grabs Stevey by the hips, and suspends half of him off the boat.

"Wash your hands. Quickly, you're so heavy," she jokes as he flicks his fingers in the water. She hoists him back onto the boat and they both turn to face me.

"I'm very impressed Rose," Jejune says.

"You got a slimy, gross one," Stevey says, his thin blonde hair moving as he giggles.

"So you know what this means, there are more fish and we'll probably catch them soon!"

"Can I try," Stevey asks.

"Come here little man." Jejune grabs the rod as Stevey climbs onto her lap. Stevey intently listens as Jejune guides his hands to the reel and explains what to look for. All his thoughts about being scared to be on a boat have vanished.

The excitement of catching my first fish leaves my body as I think about the question I was going to ask Jejune. Stevey laughs as Jejune smiles, his whole body shifting as she gives him a kiss. They are both so happy in this moment. Pure joy is emanating from them. Now is not the right time to ask. Maybe later, but not now.

The boat slowly trudges on as do the days. Each day more or less becomes the same routine. Mornings we lay out the solar batteries from Fred to charge our flashlights for nighttime. Eat, whether it is fish we catch or food from our bags. Talk nonsense, tell stories, listen to Stevey describe everything he sees in great detail; that boy has the biggest imagination. We have found clearings along the way, which we use to dock the boat. When docked we all "shower" with the water from the river and stretch out our limbs. With the time crunch of reaching the West and Counting Day approaching, we keep those rest periods short.

For tonight, Jejune takes first watch and rowing at night, and I, the second shift. Although the river is beautiful during the day, the absence of light and heightened sense of hearing in the pitch black night increase my fearfulness. Not to mention, how eerie the night is. Jejune said it is best to use the motor during the day but turn it off and paddle manually at night. The slow paddling, small source of sight from the flashlight, and being the only one awake if anything were to happen… it is unsettling. Jejune and I are fine with this continuous routine, and as is Stevey for now. For a little kid like him though, I think after four to five days of being secluded in a tiny boat with no room for activity, he is going to crack.

Per usual, Jejune takes the first night shift. The sun has finally set, leaving nothing but darkness around us. Stevey and I wiggle about to find a comfortable position for resting, which is nearly impossible. Stevey continues to struggle, quietly exhaling to himself with each readjustment. With the limited dim lighting I have to work with, I reach out for his skinny arm.

"You want to switch spots Stevey?" I ask. "I can take the middle tonight." Irritated, he brushes his wavy hair from his face and fixes his glasses.

"No I'm okay thank you Rose," he politely says back. "I want to get there already. JJ," he turns his body around rocking the boat. "Are we there yet?"

"Like I said baby, almost," she replies, pushing the paddle against the water.

"You said that yesterday," he whines.

"Stevey, I'm not going to argue. You're very tired, you need to rest."

"No I don't, I can stay up if I want to," he mumbles, turning back towards me. Stevey pulls the blanket to his chin, angrily tensing up his face. He is trying so hard, but he is too cute to come off as being angry.

"Hey," I whisper. I slide my body closer to Stevey. He continues to keep his tense face and eyes shut. "Hey Stevey," I whisper again.

"What?" he murmurs.

"I was thinking about that map you were coloring for history class." I pause, no response. "You remember the one I am talking about?"

"Yes, I was coloring it at your house next to you," he states, still eyes closed.

"Well, I was wondering if you could tell me about the West. I know nothing about it and you are really smart, could you tell me what it is going to be like?"

"You're lying," he whispers back, still eyes shut. "I'm not that smart."

"Are you crazy!" I loudly whisper. "Stevey, you are one of the smartest people I know."

"Really?" The tension in his face loosens, his eyes relaxing as they remain closed.

"Really." Stevey flashes his eyes open and pulls the blanket even closer to his chin as he begins his description.

"The West is going to be really cool," he whispers to me. "There are trees, rivers, buildings, just like we have, but even more. Miss Rebecca told us that the West has the most mountains. I've never seen a mountain. Mountains are like hills but bigger! They are taller than the trees and people used to climb them. I think it would be cool to climb a mountain…"

I continue to listen to Stevey ramble as sleep sinks into my skin. As Stevey tells his story with great excitement, I think back to when I was his age and my mom used to tell me stories when I could not sleep. She would talk of the sky, the ocean, or adventures with me as the hero. My eyes close as I begin to descend into my own dreams. I start to think of my mom and dad. I wonder if she is sleeping while dad is hard at work. I wonder if they miss me or worried that I have not called. I plan to call once we arrive in the West. Stevey's sweet voice fades away as I focus on my parents and the subtle movement from the boat, rocking me into a deep slumber.

***

Jejune nudges me awake. It is my turn to take watch and row. I stagger to the front of the boat, readjusting the flashlight to better see ahead of me. I brush the paddle against the water and swing my arm across the boat as droplets of water kiss my legs. I brush the paddle against the water again pushing the boat further. Switch, paddle, switch, paddle. This soon becomes autopilot as I try my best to see in the dark. My eyes flutter open as I try to stay awake.

Just a few more hours then Jejune will take over.

A chill runs up my body from the collection of cool water now on my legs. I decide to rest the paddle next to me, giving my arms a break and allowing my legs to dry. A yawn fills my face as the boat slowly continues down the river. The water at the front of the boat shown through the narrow path of the flashlight is still. The blanket of stars on top of the night sky takes my attention. Besides the flashlight, the hundreds of stars are the only source of light. I wonder if my dad is looking at the same stars as me at his work tonight. Reverting my attention back to the water, I notice something in the distance. I lean over the boat to get a closer look, faintly seeing what looks to be dark zigzags a few meters ahead. Vines? Tree branches?

I pick up the flashlight and extend my hand out, trying to add more light to what it is. As the boat continues to steadily move, like a rollercoaster as it approaches the peek before dropping, the zigzags become clearer. They form into intertwined pieces of rope, creating a barrier of net. I quickly secure the flashlight back on the boat and tiptoe over Stevey to wake Jejune.

"Jejune," I whisper, waving my hand to find her shoulder in the dark. "There is a barrier up ahead."

"A barrier?" she groggily asks.

"Yes, netting in the water."

"That's it." Jejune jumps awake and fumbles to get to the front of the boat. "That's the border." Crouching down to find where Stevey's body is laying, I step over him once again and follow Jejune to the front. The flashlight barely illuminates Jejune as she steers the boat to the right.

"Where are we going?" I softly ask.

"The barrier looks like it's still pretty far. That's it Rose. We've reached the edge of the Northwest." Jejune continues to furiously paddle to the right. The flashlight enlightens a handful of trees, and Jejune quickly switches to the other side, attempting to redirect the boat. The trees fade away and we are once again met with the netting not too far up ahead. "There's definitely going to be night crew at the border," she continues. "Frank told me there would be. He told me exactly what to say and how to handle them."

"Handle them? What do you mean handle them?"

"In case they get suspicious. A boat arriving to the edge during the day is normal. Could be work, could be travel. A boat arriving to the edge at night on the other hand, and after curfew, could raise some eyebrows."

This is something I did not think about. I did not think Amella would question our travel. After Jejune's continued skepticism, the mystery piece of land out West, and Frank admitting Amella killed Jejune's father, I guess I should question Amella more. I always thought I could trust them but now, now I really do not know. As Jejune expected, the flashlight shows a portion of a wooden dock. Four black boots emerge into the light, awaiting our arrival.

"Let me do the talking," Jejune states, bringing the boat to a stop. "Follow my lead. Wake up Stevey and tell him the same."

As Jejune brings the boat into the dock, I wake Stevey and tell him what is going on. He asks if he can go back to bed, but I ask him to try to stay awake. He tries to ask me more questions, but I stumble into him as the boat collides with the dock. Like the opening of a musical where all the lights blind the audience members, the boat is lit up by the two crew member's flashlights standing on the dock. Stevey crawls back under his blanket as I squint up to see Amella's usual night crew: mask, gun by their side, in all black.

"Good evening gentlemen," Jejune says, securing the rope from the boat to the dock. "I didn't realize it was daylight already." I swallow a lump of anxiety. Frank may have instructed Jejune on how to handle the night crew, but he failed to realize her unpredictable sarcasm. One of the crew members click their flashlight off.

"What brings you to the West this time of night?" the crew member with the flashlight still on asks, mask muffling their voice.

"Work purposes," Jejune states, staring straight at the crew member. Luckily for Jejune, her hat is blocking the blaring light. The crew member flashes their eyes to Jejune's hat then towards the boat.

"You do realize it is after curfew."

"Apologies," Jejune replies.

"Would you all mind stepping out of the boat." Although the water is quietly waving back and forth, it is still hard to hear the crew member through their mask.

"Is there a problem?" Jejune asks.

"Step out of the boat." Jejune stares at the crew member. After a few beats she nods her head.

"Of course," she replies. "If we may, could my friend here make sure the boat is secure as I wake up the little one? I don't want him to be startled." Both crew members are silent. "It will only take a second," Jejune reassures. The crew member moves their head slightly giving us approval to do so.

Jejune walks to Stevey and crouches down beside him. I approach the rope, pulling on it a few times to make sure it is secure. I have no clue what I am doing, and I can tell the crew member knows I do not either by their flashlight shining directly on me, illuminating my bullshit. I take my time adding one more knot to the dock, sneaking a glance at Jejune. Her face is right in front of Stevey's as she rubs his side gently. I cannot make out what she is saying but she keeps touching her ear repeatedly.

Why does she keep touching her ear?

"Hurry it up," the crew member commands. I speed up my movements and secure the knot, brushing my hands off my bare legs before standing up. The crew member moves the light towards the dock, drawing a path for me to follow. I hop onto the dock, my short hair and the boat bouncing from my jump. Jejune soon follows, carrying Stevey off the boat in her arms. As she balances his weight and hers, she steadily raises herself onto the dock to stand next to me. The crew member motions for the other crew member to search the boat. The crew member hops into the boat, their boots echoing from the vibration of the wood.

"Put the kid down," the crew member says. Jejune gingerly places Stevey's feet on the dock. He shields his eyes from the flashlight, wrapping the blanket tighter around his shoulders. "You said you were here for work purposes?" The crew member holds the light directly in Jejune's face.

"Come on man," she says, squeezing her eyes shut. "Yes, I'm here for work purposes."

"And him," he asks, the mask continuing to suppress his voice.

"My little brother. We have no parents, I couldn't leave him home alone."

"And you," the crew member shifts the light to me. "Why are you here?"

"Work purposes as well," Jejune answers.

"I didn't ask you," the crew member states, snapping the light back in Jejune's eyes. "I asked her," the crew member finishes, flicking the light back in my eyes.

"Work purposes as well," I echo through squinted eyes.

"And what is it you do for work exactly?" the crew member asks. I can faintly see the other crew member in the boat from the backlight of the flashlight. The crew member is going through our bags. I quickly search my memory for what is in our bags. Food, clothes, fishing gear, weapons. Jejune has the weapons. I try my hardest to see which bag the crew member is going through.

Please don't be Jejune's. Please don't find the weapons.

"… which is why we have the boat," Jejune continues to drone on. "We were expecting to arrive tomorrow morning, but as you can see, we arrived early."

"Hmm," the crew member responds. "I'm going to have to scan all of you, see if arriving in the West is on your schedules. Roll up your sleeves and present your wrists please."

Can they do that?

"Is that really necessary?" Jejune asks.

My vein scan will show I work in the Film Industry.

"I want to go back to bed," Stevey mumbles into his blanket.

Arriving to the West is not in my schedule.

"Sir, the boy is extremely tired," Jejune states. "We're all tired. We've been traveling –"

"Present your wrists. Now."

"We got a weapon!" the crew member on the boat exclaims through their mask. The crew member in front of us turns to see the other holding up a knife.

"Now Stevey!" Jejune yells.

Stevey covers his ears and looks down at his feet. Jejune's hand connects with the crew member's neck and he collapses to the ground as her other hand reaches for his gun. The other crew member on the boat drops the knife and reaches for their gun. Both guns go off one after the other. I drop to the ground as my ear is hit with a high pitch ringing. My entire body shakes as I fear for another shot to ring through the night. Jejune cautiously places the gun on the ground and takes the flashlight. She grabs Stevey's hands and uncovers his ears, brushing his wild, blonde hair out of his face and embracing him.

"Good boy," she says to him, the ringing in my ear making her voice seem distant and hazy. "Don't open your eyes. Turn around, count to one hundred, and don't look back until you're done." Stevey continues to squeeze his eyes shut as Jejune carefully spins him to face the other way.

"One, two, three…" Stevey counts as I clench the skin around my ear, attempting to extract the ringing from it. My chest rises and falls from my heavy breathing as I take in what just happened.

"Hey, Rose, hey," I weakly hear Jejune say. I look at the crew member lying in front of me. There is a skinny dark rod sticking out of his neck. The poison toothpick

Fred gave us.

"Rose? Rose, look at me!" Jejune yells, running to my side. My breathing becomes faster as I twist the skin on my ear harder. "Rose! Look at me! Look at me!" Jejune shouts, grabbing hold of my face with both her hands and shaking my head. "You do not have time to think about what just happened. Okay? We have to go now." My breathing remains rapid, my heartbeat pounding throughout my head. My eyes are glued to the small toothpick sticking out of the crew member's motionless neck. I can't look away. "Two shots went off. Someone was bound to hear them. We have to go now. Do you understand?"

"You–you–you killed him." I barely get the words out. My body is shaking. My face becomes hot, hotter than it has ever been before.

"Rose, look at me," she exclaims, snapping her head towards me. Her eyes burn through mine. I can feel pressure forming behind my eyes as the corners of my eyes start to become blurry. "You cannot breakdown. Hold in your tears."

I swallow, pausing my heavy breathing for a moment. I continue to look at Jejune as she holds my face. I don't know how to feel but Jejune is right, I cannot let a tear fall. I cannot lose a sphere. I try to nod as she secures her hold on my face. The pressure behind my eyes subsides and my vision becomes clearer, my breathing gradually becoming normal again.

"Help me get everything out of the boat," Jejune says, releasing her hold on my face. My cheeks sink back into their normal place. I free my ear from my grip and sniffle, sucking back up my emotions. If Jejune can get through this without crying, so can I. I have no excuse. I should be the strongest one. I am the six.

I avoid the deceased crew member on the dock as I follow Jejune. Trembling, I make my way down into the boat as Stevey's voice echoes over the open water. Thank goodness I witnessed what happened and not him. In the boat I find the other crew member floating in a pool of their own blood. They resemble the actress who was shot at Counting Day on stage: lifeless. All that can be seen of the crew member's true identity is the frozen look of fear in their eyes. My mind replaces the crew member's motionless face with the fallen actress'. How could Jejune have done this? How can she be so calm after taking another person's life. More importantly, how does she know how to shoot a gun? I continue to be hypnotized by the dead crew member. I can feel the pressure building behind my eyes and my heart rate increasing.

"Rose, help me now," Jejune snaps at me.

Avoiding the dead crew member and blood spreading from the bullet hole in their stomach, I ignore my heartbeat pounding throughout my face. I grab anything I can find and toss it onto the dock. A few solar panels are floating in the crew member's blood and my body starts to go numb again.

"JJ I finished," Stevey says, starting to turn his head towards the boat.

"Do it again!" Jejune barks at Stevey. He turns back around and begins counting from one, wrapping himself in his blanket. "Rose, we don't have much time," Jejune pressures, throwing the last of our belongings onto the dock. She takes the crew member's bloody gun, rinses it in the water, and tosses it on the dock. "Help me with him." Jejune hops out of the boat and positions herself behind the poisoned crew member back on the dock. I become frozen with fear again. "Just do it Rose," she yells towards me, beginning to grab the lifeless body.

Like a zombie, I numbly do what I am told and make my way back on the dock. Jejune removes the toothpick from his neck and, similar to flipping a tire, we struggle to roll him into the boat. My mind flashes to Jejune and I dragging Chard's body through the streets of the North. Once again, we are moving an unconscious man's body, I hope this does not become a regular activity for us. Gravity takes over as he falls off the dock and onto the other dead crew member. Jejune furiously unties the rope from the dock and gives the boat a big push back in the direction we came. I stand over Jejune watching the entire thing, utterly paralyzed.

"It's only a matter of time before someone finds the boat or alerts that crew members are missing," she says. "We have to go." Jejune lugs multiple bags on her back and grabs Stevey's hand. "Okay baby," she says, hoisting him up as he wraps his legs around her waist and stops counting. "You did a good job. Thank you for listening to JJ." Jejune hands me one of the two guns from the crew members and I stare at it blankly. She takes her gun and shoves it down the front of her pants. "I'd rather there be a good guy with a gun than a bad guy with one," she states. I continue to stare at the gun as the event flashes through my mind again: gunshots, blood, dead eyes –

"Rose," Jejune says, knocking me out of my state. Not reacting, she rolls her eyes and slaps the gun in my hand. I stare at it in my hands and my breathing picks up again. I flinch as Jejune's fingertips brush across my knuckles, closing my hand around the gun. "You don't have to use it, but we can't leave it here."

Trying my hardest to forget everything that just happened, I fumble to flick on my flashlight and walk away from the once peaceful water that is now a murder scene. I remind myself I need to stay strong as I continue further into the dark woods. With no clear path or idea of what to do next, we once again hope for the best and stick together.

I never thought I could hate a food so much. If it wasn't for Jejune grabbing the cooler off the boat, I don't know what we would be eating. I guess I should be thankful, but I'm sick of fish. Not to mention camping in the woods. I miss my bed.

"JJ can I go find some rocks?" Stevey asks.

"Finish up your last bit of food then you can," she says, kissing him on the forehead. I don't understand how they can think everything is okay. In Stevey's defense he didn't see or hear any of it, but as for Jejune, she has no excuse, she *killed* two people. "Don't go too far." Stevey runs off behind us.

I place my fish on a stick over our small lit fire, heating it up some more, even though I don't have much of an appetite.

"Rose you have to eat something." Ignoring her words, I continue to twirl my fish. Jejune exhales, putting her fish down. "Rose you have to stop."

"Stop? It's like a nonstop loop in my mind," I say, twirling my stick faster.

"I know there isn't anything I'm going to say to make it go away, but you have to understand, they were going to kill us."

"You don't know that."

"Yeah I do Rose. You don't know what these people are capable of." Jejune grabs her fish and yanks off a piece of meat with her teeth. "Just remember what all this is for." I start to spin my stick faster and faster. "You have to move on and get over it." Fed up, I fling the stick from my hands into the fire.

"We were taught many things when we were younger, but we weren't taught

142

how to deal with your friend stabbing and shooting people right in front of you." I stand up, pacing with my thoughts. "How do you even know how to shoot a gun?"

"But we were taught how to deal with death," Jejune rebuttals.

"And we were taught to trust Amella."

"And look where that's gotten us," Jejune says presenting her arms out. Her comment hangs in the trees as we look at one another. Jejune brings her hands to her face and starts to laugh. "Why do I even try? You know what Rose, I guess you're just never gonna get it."

"JJ!" Stevey emits with his tiny voice running back to us, hair flopping all around. "JJ," he says again with barely any breath. "I thought doors were supposed to be on a house."

"They usually are," she responds.

"Then," Stevey takes another breath. "Why is there one in the ground?" Jejune takes in the question, her face becoming serious.

"Show me." Assassinating the fire with her boot, she stomps out the heat and light. Stevey tugs on Jejune's arm like a dog leading its owner during a walk and I quickly grab all our bags and follow suit. His excited feet kick up the dirt in his path as he continues to lead the way and ramble on.

"I thought it was a big rock but then I couldn't pick it up. Well, I can't pick up big rocks anyway, but then I realized there was an identical one right next to it. Then I saw those tiny metal things like we have on the side of our doors and then I thought it must be a door."

"Wow, that was a lot little man," Jejune replies, a hint of worry in her voice. He stops walking, making Jejune and I halt in our tracks. He looks up at Jejune.

"I know, I wanted to tell you everything. I wanted to bring you up to speed."

"I've never heard you say that phrase before," Jejune remarks.

"Fred taught it to me when we were working." Stevey turns back forward and keeps walking. After some more steps, we reach our destination. "I didn't open the door because you told me I can't go in places I don't know."

"Thanks for listening to your big sister," Jejune says with a smile.

The door is small but Stevey was not wrong, upon first glance, I would think it was two identical rocks. The doorframe blends with the surrounding cinnamon colored dirt, except for the iron hinges and jagged rock door handles. "What do you think is in it?" Stevey asks, looking at the both of us.

"I don't know," Jejune replies softly, looking around. "But let's find out." She bends down and flings one of the doors open as Stevey and I back up, fearful something may emerge. Jejune holds the door open, looks to what's inside, and then to us. "Shall we?" Stevey and I peer our heads over the gaping hole to see a long set of stairs leading into darkness.

"JJ it looks scary," Stevey timidly says, recoiling towards her body.

"That's why Rose and I are here to protect you." Jejune reaches around her back for her flashlight and lifts up her shirt to grab the concealed gun.

"No," I react, placing my hand on hers. Using Jejune's own words, I continue. "What if someone thinks we are the bad guy with the gun." Jejune takes in my comment and lifts her shirt back up, shoving the gun back down her pants.

"Touché," she smiles. "Hold onto me and don't let go unless I say so." Stevey nods and squeezes her shirt with both hands, as if his life depends upon it. Jejune clicks on the flashlight, revealing dirt and mold suffocating the staircase. She adjusts her hat and lets out a long exhale. "Here goes nothing."

I follow them down the narrow stairs with my flashlight. Chunks of gravel are peeling and there is a musky smell in the air; nothing like the marble steps in North Amella. As we travel further down, I notice pieces of the railing are torn off, leaving splintered edges. It's obvious someone has been here, and may still be here. The stairs take a sharp right turn and with a few more cautious steps we reach a landing. We are met with a dull wall and what looks to be a drawing of a girl. She has a tight pink shirt on and what resembles fuchsia ruffles like a bird's nest around her waist. She is balancing on the tips of her toes with shoes I have never seen before, almost rectangular in shape, with ribbon tying up her ankles.

"What is she doing?" Stevey asks.

"She's dancing," a hoarse voice to the left of us shouts. Startled, Jejune and I rotate our flashlights to the source of the voice as Stevey hides for cover behind us. "Damn, you all look rough," a thin Asian woman with long silver hair matching her six spheres under her eyes says. "Check them for weapons." She crosses her arms as two other figures emerge behind her. The others come closer to the light and become more visible. They are two Asian boys a little over Stevey's age. Jejune swiftly reveals her gun and points it at the two boys who stop dead in their tracks. Silence fills the room but is shattered by the slow clapping of the woman with the silver hair.

"I got to admit," she says, ceasing her applause. "By the looks of you, I did not think you would have weapons, let alone a gun." She makes her way in between the boys and to us. "But I've learned to never judge solely on appearance," she concludes with a smirk. She is standing directly in front of Jejune, the gun inches away from her chest. "Would you mind," the woman calmly asks. Jejune lowers the gun, placing it back in her waist. They both stare at one another for some time. "Nice scar, that your son?" she asks, peering over Jejune's shoulder.

"Don't look at him," Jejune snaps. The woman's eyebrows raise, taken aback by Jejune's response.

"And who are you?" she asks me, still staring at Jejune.

"We're not looking to get to know each other," Jejune intervenes.

"I like you. Feisty." The woman smiles, a smooth wall of white teeth flashing. "Not enough of you left."

"Tell me about it," Jejune responds.

"The name is Jean," the woman reveals. "Those youngsters are Watson and Johnny."

"Jejune, Rose, Stevey," Jejune informs.

"Pleasure. Come in and meet the others." The woman, who I now know is Jean, turns around and begins to walk. Her bone straight hair reaches her butt, bouncing with each step, like the mane on a horse. Watson and Johnny rush down the hall.

"How do we know this isn't a trap," Jejune inquires.

"You're the one with a gun aren't you? Just shoot if anything happens," Jean says over her shoulder.

After a few steps, Jean flicks a switch and the place comes to life. Jejune and I take in our surroundings and click off our flashlights. A banana colored hallway is filled with photographs like the first drawing we saw. Some with women, some with men. A woman and man embracing, a woman leaping in the air, another touching her feet to her head. The photographs and frames are perfect and clean, unlike everything else surrounding the place.

We are soon met with a large room where clothes and towels are hanging from long poles mounted to the walls. One wall is a huge mirror, many sections stamped with oily handprints. The room is dimly lit with candles and scarce overhead lighting. Mats and sleeping bags are all piled together underneath a handful of people forming an island of comfort. And finally, a polished piano in the corner just like the perfectly kept photographs; seems so out of place.

"We got guests," Jean announces to the group of people milling about. Watson, Johnny, and herself join the others sitting on the ground.

"How lovely," a pretty girl exclaims.

"We don't need any more people Jean," a kid with bright red hair grunts.

"Yeah Jean," a boy Stevey's age adds.

"Shut up the both of you," an older man says.

"Make me you old fart!" the red haired kid hisses. They all begin to talk over one another as Jejune, Stevey, and I continue to stand before them. Jean looks to us.

"Guess they don't want to meet you," she says with a short shoulder shrug.

"I do!" the pretty girl innocently sings.

"The one with the hat has a gun!" Watson shouts and everyone falls silent. "And they don't know what a dancer is."

"Great, we got your attention," Jean says. "This is Jejune, Rose, and Stevey."

"Sweet hat!" the old man says to Jejune. "Where can I get one of those?"

"Screw the hat," the red haired kid scoffs. "Where can I get a gun?" The pretty girl raises her hand and speaks.

"Can we all introduce ourselves? Hi, my name is Violet and it is very nice to meet you," she says sincerely.

"Would you stop with this nice crap," the red haired kid cries. "Name's Sid."

"Lawrence," the older man states. "Welcome."

"I'm Charlie," the boy Stevey's age says.

"Johnny, we met earlier." Jejune and I nod in recognition.

"Watson, we also met earlier."

We all look to the last person. She is a girl, about Jejune and I's age, avoiding eye contact and hunched over.

"You gonna speak or what?" Sid says. She begins rubbing her neck as her eyes flicker like an insect's wings flapping. Besides Sid, everyone else looks to her in an encouraging manner. The girl looks back at the ground and softly replies.

"Pearl."

Mockingly, Sid dramatically claps and Johnny and Watson start hitting him, getting him to quit.

"It's not the best bunch but it's the bunch we got," Jean replies. "I'd invite you all to sit but you honestly look like shit." Instinctually, Stevey covers his ears. "Oh, apologies, what I mean is, you're welcome to use our showers. Freshen up if you would like."

"Seriously?" Jejune asks, looking to everyone for reassurance.

"You would be doing us a favor," Sid says disgusted, gesturing to the wall of mirrors. On cue, we all turn and finally see ourselves for the first time since our travels through the woods. I am caked in mud, smeared with dirt, and can barely see my skin. Although we bathed occasionally down the river, there is no evidence of that occurring. I don't even recognize myself. I have become so unpolished.

"Please, before Jean changes her mind," Lawrence says, the rest making noises in agreement.

"On one condition," Jean interrupts. "You tell us how you got a gun."

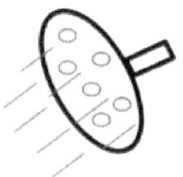

We tell them the entire story from the beginning. Jejune's suspicion, the old man shooting the actress, Stevey crying, getting lost in the woods, killing the crew members; everything. Jejune does not however mention Fred or Frank. They all listen in awe like the climactic scene of a movie.

"What an incredible story," Violet smiles. "Violent, but incredible."

"It's a dumb story," Sid scoffs. "They don't even have a plan. They found us by accident."

"Look who's talking," Lawrence gargles, Sid regretfully looking down.

"Thank you for sharing. It means a lot that you can trust us," Jean states.

"Thanks for taking us in," Jejune replies. Jean turns to look at everyone.

"Violet." She springs up beaming, ready for her order. "Go get the showers ready." Violet nods and rushes out of the room. "Johnny and Watson, grab towels and toiletries from the back room." Both of the boys turn to one another and high five. "And *only* grab the towels and toiletries," Jean firmly states. Defeated, the boys make their way out of the room. "Sid, take Charlie to go get clean clothes for them."

"No need, we have –" Jean waves her hand up, silencing my voice. Sid and Jean stare at one another. "Now," she commands. Sid rolls his eyes.

"Charlie," he shouts across the room. Stevey and Charlie stop playing with the toys in the corner. "Come on," he says with a nudge of his head. Charlie runs over to Sid as Stevey runs back to Jejune. Jean gives Lawrence an apologetic look as he makes his way over to Pearl. He carefully puts his arm around her and whispers in her ear, her eyes still wild and frightened. Jean faces the three of us again, swooping her long, misty gray hair back off her shoulder.

"Take as long as you would like. We only have two showers available, but I am sure you two," she gestures to Stevey and Jejune, "would not mind sharing. Dinner will be served within the hour."

"We really can't thank you enough Jean," Jejune sincerely says.

"No need to thank me. It's what we do for good people." Good people? We broke the rules and killed two crew members. Took the lives of two innocent people. How does that make us good?

Johnny and Watson return chasing one another as Violet briskly walks in to let us know the showers are ready. Violet leads us to where the showers are, which are surprisingly in great condition. Like the stairs we walked down to get here, I thought the mold and debris would have found its way to here as well.

"If it gets too hot, just turn it to the right," Violet energetically says.

"They know how to use a shower airhead," Sid mocks, coming around the corner.

"Just," Violet tries to hold her smile, even though she is upset. "Just yell if you need anything," she says, rushing off.

"You know, you don't have to be so mean," Jejune states, taking her boots off. Sid looks at her, rage in his eyes.

"Here are your clothes freak," he says throwing them at her. "How did you even get that scar anyway?" Jejune stops untying her boots and unfolds her spine to an upright position. She slowly approaches Sid, getting closer to his face, their noses practically touching.

"I can show you how." Swallowing his fear, Sid picks his chin up higher, keeping eye contact.

"Good luck trying to get the dirt off you." Sid whips my clean clothes at me and walks away.

"Punk," Jejune says, going back to taking her boots off. Jejune gets both her socks off and then looks at me. "You gonna shower or what?"

"Yeah." I look to her, fidgeting with the pile of clean clothes in my hands. "I don't know, don't you think this is weird?"

"Last time I checked, showering isn't weird," she replies, helping Stevey undress.

"Not that," I reply. "Letting us take a shower. They don't even know us."

"They're nice people," Jejune shrugs, standing to start the shower.

"I guess so." I think about it some more but then snap out of it, I too, beginning to take my shoes and socks off. Jejune motions for Stevey to enter as she looks to me again.

"I know when we were younger, Amella taught us the right way to treat strangers and that was to not treat them in anyway, just to act like they are strangers. But maybe Amella's way of treating people isn't the only way, or the right way." Jejune steps into the shower, getting fully naked in private. I finish undressing and step into the rectangular space.

The water is so soothing on my exhausted skin. I sink my head down and watch the dirt trickle down and off my body. I hear Jejune and Stevey leave, but I stay in the shower a while longer, enjoying the cleanse. After a long and well needed detox, I crank the shower off and reach around for my towel. I pat myself dry, secure the towel around my breasts, and drag the shower curtain open. Two hands make me move backwards and pin me against the shower wall as I try to step out.

"Where are you hiding it," Sid demands, his hands holding me back.

"What?" I ask, fumbling to keep myself covered.

"Don't play dumb with me Rose, Jejune said she killed two crew members and she has a gun which means you have the other so I'm gonna ask you again." He nudges his face closer. "Where are you hiding it?"

"Get your hands off me or I'll scream." I try my best to keep my composure. His hot breath is spreading across my face as I look away. The fire in his eyes matches his cherry hair.

"Tell me!" he insists, pressing deeper into my shoulders. Just as I am about to scream, Sid is thrown backwards out of the shower. Jean grabs the collar of his jacket, forcing him to look at her but he looks away, like a dog when they know they have done something bad.

"Did he hurt you?" Jean asks, looking towards me. I shake my head, still clenching the towel around me. "Who do you think you are, hmm?" Jean says, directing her attention back to Sid. "What did we tell you when we took you in?"

"Hands," Sid peeps.

"What?" Jean pulls his collar more firmly.

"Hands to ourselves," Sid mumbles, his voice full of embarrassment.

"So listen to what we say. You want to go back, is that what you want."

"No!" Sid cries, his one sphere bulging out at Jean. "No, please!"

"Then listen." Jean loosens her grip on him and pushes him back. He quickly looks to me, an apology swarming in his eyes as he runs away. I relax my shoulders and adjust my stance. Jean exhales as she reaches down to hand me my clothes. "I apologize for his actions."

"It's okay," I say, taking the clothes from her.

"He is threatened by you just like he is threatened by me. Unlike him, you and I have something in common." We look at one another, our six spheres reflecting each other's. We both do not say anything, but we do not need to exchange words to know why he is threatened. We are sixes. We have strength, and more importantly, we have power. "My husband Lawrence and I, we wanted a way out. Since Amella owns everything, we knew we would die on our own without them. So, Lawrence transferred all his points to me so I could keep us going. We found Pearl and Sid in the woods. Both were badly beaten with only one sphere left." I continue to clench my towel as I begin to shiver from the cool air. "Sid has much resentment for Amella and the world in general, but Pearl, she hasn't recovered. She won't speak to anyone, not even Sid. We don't know what she has been through, but all we can do is feed her and give her a place to stay. Violet, she's our newest. She is still brainwashed, thinks the world is just dandy. I guess you could say we've made a safe home for kids like them." I continue to listen, confused as to why she is telling me all this.

"Johnny, Watson, and Charlie are our own, and we raise them well, even though they are threes. I don't see them as threes though, I see them as my strong boys. Just like how I don't see you and I as sixes. We are so much more than just a number." She pauses and I watch as Jean gets lost in her own thoughts. "Although we're all here in the West, Lawrence and I raised the boys in the North. We couldn't tell anyone we left so technically I am still a Northerner." Jean stops, looking directly at me. "I saw it too. That old man shooting the actress on stage. I was in the same ballroom as you. The screaming, the gunshots, the crying. Imagine, sixes crying. We're supposed to be the strong ones." Jean starts to laugh, as if the idea of sixes shedding tears is ridiculous. "My point is Rose, do you really think those little dots under your eyes define who you are?"

That's a question that has been asked a lot of me lately, and the more I keep getting asked, the more confused I am. Jean lets out a huge exhale as she looks at me, still shivering in the shower gripping my towel.

"Dinner is ready," she says. "Get dressed quickly before all the others leave you no food. We weren't expecting three more mouths to feed tonight."

I clutch my towel and hold my clothes until Jean leaves. Like a teardrop, I slide down the shower wall, sitting in a pile of cold water. Why is everyone questioning me? Why is everyone convinced what we were taught all our lives is a lie? My body swells with that feeling I got on the boat dock. Heavy breathing, heart beating, pressure behind my eyes. I do not care what anyone says. I am a six, I have always been a six, and I plan to stay a six. What is so wrong with that.

I snap out of that state of mind and slip into the new clothes I was given. They are a little baggy and not my style but they work. Grabbing my dirty clothes, I find my way back into the main room. Jejune, Stevey, and all the others are helping themselves to the food that has been brought.

"Don't worry," Lawrence calls to me. "Aster is getting the other load of food."

"Violet," Jean says, brushing her hair from her face. "Could you go see if Aster needs any help?" She nods and runs past me. "Rose put your stuff down and help yourself please." I join the others as they pick what they can. Jejune hands me a plate. There are berries, plants, what looks to be cooked meat, and my new least favorite dish: fish. Hesitant, I reach for some berries and a piece of meat.

"Look what Aster brought today!" Violet says, racing back into the room. Violet is holding two bags of sliced bread and trailing behind her is a familiar face holding a bag of sugar cookies. Buzzed blonde hair, muddy brown eyes, two spheres, and cheeks sprinkled with freckles. Our eyes meet and it does not take long for both of us to realize we know one another.

"Sugar cookies!" Stevey and Charlie yell in unison. They both run towards Aster as greediness fills their eyes. Aster hands over the bag without a fight.

"I see we have newcomers," she comments, taking off her shoes and jacket. Her voice is just like how she speaks in front of the camera, warm and calming.

"I apologize for my little brother ambushing you," Jejune says, rolling her eyes. "He is Stevey, I am Jejune," she says, tipping her hat.

"Rose, nice to meet you," I say. I quickly turn around to grab utensils, not knowing how she is going to react to the situation.

"Well, it is nice to officially meet you," Aster says. The room falls silent as mystery swirls in the air.

"Officially?" Sid questions.

"What does officially mean?" Charlie asks, adding some comic relief to the room.

"It means that they have now formally met," Sid announces with a pile of berries in his mouth. "Nonetheless, you've met?" I glance towards Jejune who is looking at me questionably. I look back at Aster, who is grinning.

"Wait, do you think like, you're in trouble or something?" She starts laughing and shakes her head. "Always with their guards up. I swear it is a six thing," she says, looking to Jean, who is holding her hands up in a surrender fashion. "Rose and I," Aster continues, putting her arm around me, "have met during the magic hour. Sound person," she states pointing to me. "Actress," she says, pointing to herself. The others nod and mumble in agreement.

Unfazed, everyone goes back to normal, chatting, eating, and being in their own little worlds. Aster still has her arm around me as I uncomfortably smile at her. She flashes that enticing smile. Even in this dimly lit room, it is still as beautiful as it is on the screen.

"It's an honor to finally meet my North sound boom technician after all this time." She takes her arm off me and helps herself to the food she has brought back for everyone. All this time? How many times has she seen me on set? Have I really never noticed her before? Aster may be the actress but she is nothing like the girl I saw that day. She is so happy and vocal, not at all like the saddened face that walked by me off the set. Maybe she was just having a bad day when our eyes met? I am so confused. This whole day has been one big lump of confusion. Feeling dizzy, I plop down next to Jejune, who is almost finished with her meal.

"Hey miss didn't-realize-you-had-so-many-friends," Jejune jokes. I chuckle, trying not to seem as overwhelmed as I feel on the inside.

"Aster what did you do today?" Violet cheerfully asks.

"Today," she starts, sitting next to Pearl wrapped in a blanket not speaking. She balances the plate on her lap as one hand scoops food and the other softly rubs Pearl's back. "We went over my schedule and I had a wardrobe fitting."

"That is so cool. I want to be an actress one day," Violet says, full of hope.

"We know you tell us every, single, day," Sid groans. "Besides, it will never happen."

"Sid," Aster chimes in. "If that is Violet's dream then that is Violet's dream."

"Well it is not an easy job Violet, remember that," Sid states.

"Sid we all have dreams, some are just more elaborate than others," Aster replies. I watch as she takes a tiny scoop off her plate. She hovers the spoon in front of Pearl's mouth and she cautiously takes the food.

"Momma, can we go in the big room and play now?" Watson asks to Jean.

"Clean your plates and put them on the table. Violet and Sid go and watch them please." Johnny, Watson, and Charlie run out of the room with their plates. Sid hands Violet his plate, which she kindly takes. With the motion of a sloth, Sid finally gets up and leaves.

"Can I go!" Stevey asks, nearly breaking his neck to watch the others leave.

"Finish all your food first," Jejune replies.

"So Rose and I have met, Jejune and Stevey was it?" Aster asks. Jejune shakes her head as she swallows the food in her mouth.

"Good memory," Jejune says.

"Well, I am an actress," Aster replies, feeding Pearl some more.

"I have to give you props," Jejune states. "I don't know how you can remember all those lines for the announcements."

"Luckily, those lines are on a monitor for me to read." Aster gives Pearl one more spoonful before Lawrence delicately grabs her shoulders and both make their way out of the room. Suddenly, Stevey's eyes get wide as he rapidly nudges Jejune on the arm. He crawls up to her face and whispers in her ear.

"Go ahead," Jejune whispers to Stevey. He looks around as his shoulder rises to hide himself, like a bird using its wing as a shield. Jejune exhales and looks to Aster. "My little brother wants to ask you a question."

Aster places her plate down and focuses her attention on Stevey. She flashes her beautiful smile again. Stevey looks away and shakes his head.

"Don't worry, I'm not going to bite you," Aster replies with a cute laugh.

Stevey looks back up and searches in Jejune's eyes for reassurance. Once he has gotten such he looks back to Aster.

"Are you," he readjusts his glasses and scratches his nose. "Are you the actress on TV? The one I always see?"

"Why yes I am," Aster replies.

"But, why do you look different?" Stevey asks confused.

"Well when I'm on TV I have fake hair, fake eyes, and a lot of makeup."

"So," Stevey's face scrunches with uncertainty. "The girl on TV isn't real?"

"She's real," Aster smiles. "She's right here. She just looks different."

"The girl on TV looks really pretty."

"I know. I wish I could look like her every day. Then I would be pretty all the time." Aster's smile starts to fade as she nervously blinks her feelings away. Stevey straightens to his knees, stands up, and walks over to Aster. He reaches Aster and places his tiny palm on her cheek.

"I still think you're pretty," Stevey says. Aster looks at him and brings her hand to meet the one on her face. She smiles and squeezes his small fingers. Her eyes become glossy as she lets out a laugh.

"Thank you Stevey," she softly replies. He smiles back at her, sharing the moment. He lets his hand fall off her cheek and looks back to Jejune.

"Can I go now?" he asks.

"I guess you can go now," Jejune smirks. Stevey runs out of the room, leaving just the three of us girls.

"What a sweet boy," Aster says. I look to her and notice a single tear rolling across her cheek, the stream of water playing connect the dots with her freckles. "That's the nicest thing anyone has ever said to me."

Puzzled by her reaction, I continue to watch as another tear pools over her eye, and like others who I have seen cry before, a sphere under her eye vanishes, leaving her with only one.

"Looks like I am down another sphere. I am such a crybaby," Aster jokes, laughing off her emotions. Aster may have only one sphere now, but I can tell she has a good heart. Maybe Jean was right, maybe spheres do not determine who we are.

Just like we did for the others, we retell the story of how we got here to Aster. She listens intently as the candles continue to burn around us; asking questions along the way, nodding when she understands, and widening her eyes at the shocking parts.

"Yes but why did you leave in the first place?" Aster questions.

"What do you mean?" Jejune asks.

"Why this way. Why travel west?" Jejune and I look at one another. We told everyone our story, but we never told anyone about the unknown piece of land.

"Well," I begin to say. "Have you ever been in North Amella?"

"No, I only do outside shoots, and I'm a Westerner so I stay here for Counting Day," Aster replies.

"One day, I was filming at North Amella and I noticed a map in there that did not match the map we were all taught growing up. It had an extra piece of land out West that I did not recognize."

"Like a long piece of land bordering the West," Jejune adds.

"Exactly," I agree. "I told Jejune about it so we decided to see if it was real." Aster stares at us, not saying anything. "You think we are crazy don't you?"

"Not at all. I mean, actually, it's quite possible," Aster replies. "The woods stretch on for miles, even past the edge of the West. That's probably the land you saw on the map."

"Then why would no one know about it?" I ask.

"I wouldn't put it past Amella to hide something like that," Aster blatantly states.

"They hide a lot of things," Jejune mumbles.

"So, when are you planning on getting to this unknown place."

"We left a little after last Counting Day and we were hoping to get there before the next one," Jejune says. "Once Counting Day comes and we aren't there for check in, Amella will come looking for us."

"And there will be consequences for our absence," I add.

"Then you guys better head out in the morning," Aster states.

"Why? Is something going on then?" I ask.

"Before the next Counting Day you said, right?" Aster questions again. "That's in two days."

"What?" Jejune says, fear filling her eyes.

"The next Counting Day is in two days," Aster repeats. It feels as though an avalanche is passing directly through me, twisting and crashing through all my organs and my stomach.

"No no no," Jejune nervously laughs. "No, that can't be. We've calculated the days. Kept track of the days…" Jejune presses her hands against her hat.

"You guys have to leave soon if you don't want to get caught," Aster says.

"What?" I say.

"If you want to make it before Counting Day, you have to go tomorrow, or even tonight," Aster insists.

"We can't go tonight. No one can go out tonight, or any night." I can feel my heart beating faster. My palms fill with sweat as I realize the grave mistake Jejune and I have made. I know I should say something but I can't. The feelings I got on the dock are creeping back up again as my mind fills with thoughts. There is not enough time to make it back, and if we tried to go back now, all this would be for nothing. We can't stay here because crew members will come looking, and what about the crew members we killed? Did we leave anything that would lead Amella to know we did it? That I did it? That I was a part of this? What will happen to us?

"Jejune, what are we going to do?" I muster out of my trembling body.

"I don't know Rose!" Jejune shouts, still clenching her hat.

"No," Aster says. "No we are going to get you out of here. No need to panic. If there really is a place, not run by Amella, then we'll find it." Aster looks at the both of us, her face and tone of voice becoming more serious. "I'm going to get you guys there."

"Yeah right," Jejune releases her grip on her head scoffing at Aster's speech. "How you gonna manage that?"

"I have an idea," Aster smirks.

Fear of getting caught by Amella for not reporting to Counting Day, we hear Aster out.

"I know where the edge of the West is," Aster says. "I'm willing to take you guys there after my filming tomorrow."

"You're filming in the West?" I ask.

"I'll be filming the wonderful Counting Day announcement," Aster replies with sarcasm. "The same one you did sound for last month."

"But that was in the North," I say.

"Yeah they send me all over," she scoffs, waving her hand. "I don't get much say as an actress. Luckily tomorrow I'll be filming in two locations, one really close to here and one not too far from the edge of the West."

"Okay, so what are you suggesting?" Jejune inquires. Aster readjusts her sitting position as a smile forms across her face. You can feel the excitement coming off her body.

"I know the West extremely well due to filming all over and getting the food from around here." Jejune and I nod and follow where she is going. "Because of that, I can lead you guys to exactly where the West ends and this so called unknown land begins. However, there is one problem." Aster's smile shrinks as she looks to us.

"What's the problem?" Jejune begs.

"I have to film tomorrow." Jejune's posture sinks as she realizes that is a huge problem. I look to both of them, trying to think of alternatives in my mind but Aster cuts me to the chase. "So here's my thought. Why don't I go with Stevey and one of you and the other takes my place?" Jejune and I stare at her in silence, both completely perplexed by her idea. "Just think about it," she exclaims. "You three can't go on your own, you don't know the West or how to get to the edge. You may be able to find it but probably not in enough time, these woods are like a maze, but I do know the way and I can get you there tomorrow. So one of you takes my place for filming and we will do a switch at the second filming location." Aster's smile is back as she exhales, winded from her speech. "What do you think?"

"It's a little crazy," Jejune frowns and nods her head. "But it might work," she replies with a laugh. Still trying to go through the plan in my head, I keep my mouth shut.

"Rose what do you think?" Aster asks.

"Um, I think –"

"It's a horrific idea," Jean states from behind me, finishing my thought. Aster looks up as Jejune and I turn around to see Jean standing in the doorframe with her arms crossed. "But it just may work," she adds, walking towards us. "It'll be tricky and if you get caught it's over. I don't even want to think about what Amella will do to you guys." Jean is standing over all of us, her hair washing over her like a silver waterfall. "So, who's willing to buzz their hair and dye it blonde to play the role of Aster for a day," Jean asks with a smirk.

"What?" I ask.

"If one of you is going to pretend to be Aster, you have to *look* like Aster," Jean states. "I said it would be tricky."

"Well I'm out," Jejune laughs. She looks to everyone as we await her reason. "First off, Stevey isn't going to travel *anywhere* without me by his side, and second," Jejune grabs the front of her hat and takes it off. We all stare in silence as Jejune reveals a bald head with a handful of dirty blonde hair patches sticking out like tuffs of grass. "Alopecia. I cannot grow hair." Jejune lets everyone take a good look before forcefully putting her hat back on her head.

As a long time friend of Jejune, I knew about her alopecia. She does not just wear her JJ hats to defy Amella, but to cover up her balding head. She already gets talked about for her scar and that's enough. I swallow a gulp of fear, realizing I am the one who will have to be Aster.

"Then it's decided," Jean states. "I'll get the buzzers."

"I'll grab the dye kit," Aster says, getting up.

"Jejune." My heart starts to pound in my eardrums. "I can't go through with this."

"You don't really have a choice. It's this or we get caught," Jejune states.

"I feel like I never have a choice," I exclaim. "I didn't even want to do this. My life was fine before all this adventure nonsense."

"Fine?" Jejune's eyes widen. "You think your life was fine? Rose, you did the same thing every day and let Amella dictate what you could and could not do. Where to eat, what to eat, how many points to spend, when to work –"

"So didn't you Jejune," I defend.

"Yeah but I wanted to leave so I did!"

"You wouldn't have left if I didn't see that map," I defend. "You wouldn't even be here if it wasn't for *my* points paying for everything."

"Then why did you see that map? You think that was just an accident?"

"Maybe." I can feel my breathing becoming more rapid. I try to calm myself down. "I think –"

"No Rose," Jejune firmly states, cutting me off. "There's no such thing as accidents, don't you get it." Frustrated, Jejune stands up and begins to pace. "You know what," she says, stopping with her hands on her hips. "You're just the type of person that's gonna do what they want to do when they're ready to do it. So if you're not ready to do this, then go home because you don't even care." Jejune brushes past me heading to the door.

"If I didn't care Jejune I wouldn't be here right now," I stutter, standing up to face her.

"Nah, you don't care about this." She shakes her head with her back towards me. "You don't care about the truth, you don't care about me, you don't care about Stevey." Jejune pauses, turning around to face me. Her bloodshot eye and fiery scar mingle with the anger and disappointment in her face. "You're a stereotypical selfish six. The only thing you care more about than you, is you."

Jejune walks away leaving me in a room full of tension. Attacked by Jejune's words, my mind swirls with thoughts. I think of my parents and how scared they must be that I am not home or checked in like I promised. I think of the two crew members lying dead, eyes wide open with fear. My thoughts begin to consume me as I collapse to the ground. I think of how exhausted I am from running and running and running. My chest inflates in and out as I struggle on all fours to make my mind stop. Through blurry vision I can faintly see a droplet of water splash against the hardwood floor, exploding with delight. My throat closes and I choke on the air. And for the first time in my life, I hear myself attempt to speak through heavy breathing, drawn out sniffles, and water leaking onto my face as I shake. And for the first time in my life, I let myself do something I have never done. I finally let myself cry.

Jean and Aster return to find me an emotional wreck. Unlike the group of people frozen surrounding Stevey when he cried, they both drop to the floor and come to my aid. They comfort and console me as I let myself be free and feel all my emotions. After what feels like a lifetime, Jean helps me into the bathroom, washing my face and making the tenderness around my eyes subside. I can't help to think if this is how my mom would react if I had a breakdown.

Jean lets me be and tells me to come out for my haircut when I am ready. I stare at the sink, afraid to see myself in the mirror. I know my reflection will be different. Like ripping a band aid, I snap my head up and look. My face is flushed and my eyes are puffy. The skin under and in the corner of my eyes is swollen and pink. My eyelashes are glued together from my tears and my nose is saturated with a mixture of tears and snot. The strangest thing of all is my spheres. My whole life I have always had six white circles under my eyes, but now, I have only five white circles under my eyes. Curious, I bring my fingers to where my sixth sphere used to be and rub over the area. What used to feel like a small bump has transformed to just regular, smooth skin. I am entranced with the feeling, watching my finger move back and forth in the mirror.

"You doing okay in there Rose?" Aster asks through the door.

"Yes, I'll be right out." I retract my fingers from my face as if I have been caught. I stare at my new face, taking it all in before my hair is shaved and dyed. I open the door to hear the sound of a piano playing. I follow the melody back into the large room which is now completely dark except for a few candles by the piano. Closing his eyes and swaying his head with the music, Lawrence swiftly moves his hands to create the relaxing tune that is filling the air.

"Lawrence always plays the children a song before bed," Jean smiles, popping out of the darkness. I make out what looks to be lumps of blankets to actually be all the others getting comfortable for bed. "Come on," Jean whispers, gently touching my back. "Let's go give you a haircut."

***

Lawrence's sweet tune is drowned out by the incessant buzzing of the clippers. Wanting it to be a surprise, Jean has faced me away from the mirror. As she gets the back of my head, I watch as my hair parachutes to the floor like autumn leaves floating off a tree. Although my hair is already short by Amella standards, I am still anxious about what a full buzz cut will look like on me. The buzzing stops as Jean unplugs the device. She walks in front of me and raises my chin up. A huge smile beams on her face.

"You look like a totally different person."

"She just looks like me with brown hair," Aster says.

"No she does not," Jean hastily replies. "Every individual is unique and beautiful in their own way." Jean leans in so only I can hear. "You're a very brave young lady."

"Thank you," I say, my voice nasally from crying earlier. Jean turns around and pats Aster on the back who is mixing the dye.

"You're up. You girls have fun now," Jean says, leaving us in the bathroom.

"There's no need to worry," Aster reassures, thoroughly mixing the bowl. "I know what I'm doing." Aster takes the brush out of the bowl and strokes it across my head. The dye is very cold against my scalp and has a thick consistency. Within no time, Aster slathers all the dye over my head. "It has to set for a while then I'll be back to wash it out."

"Thanks." I remain still, the numbness of my body morphing with my now damp scalp.

"You're free to move around," Aster laughs as she cleans up the mess.

"I think I will stay in here."

"Suit yourself." Aster turns and points directly at me. "But no peeking."

"I promise," I say with a small smile. Aster nods and leaves, closing the door behind her. Left alone with my own thoughts, I am too weak to move. Wetness fills my nostrils as tears flood my tired eyes. A knock on the door extinguishes my feelings. I forcefully blink away the water crowding my eyes.

"Need some company?" Jejune asks, holding the door open. Without answering, she steps into the bathroom and shuts the door. She leans up against the wall and crosses her arms, observing my new look. Not being able to contain it any longer, Jejune heaves over and bursts into laughter.

"Thanks," I state, rolling my eyes.

"I'm sorry." She covers her mouth. "You look ridiculous." Her laughter becomes contagious as I start giggling myself.

"Well, I haven't seen it yet," I reply still giggling.

"Oh boy, then you're in for a real treat." Our laughing ceases and Jejune clears her throat. "I guess an apology is in order for berating you, but on the plus side, it's good to know that you do have a soul. Welcome to the five club." We both smile at that comment. "In all seriousness, I hope you know that this means a lot." Jejune stops her talking and grins, her tone getting serious. "Even if there isn't someplace, this has been an amazing adventure, even during the scary times. I can't speak for Stevey, but he has had more excitement in the last couple weeks than his entire life. I've never seen him smile so much." Jejune takes a moment to stop and look at me. "Thank you Rose."

"You know we both did this Jejune, I can't take all the credit." I look to her, my eyes still feeling puffy. "You were just so damn convincing I couldn't resist."

"Yeah that was it," Jejune laughs at my attempt to lie through my teeth. "Like that time I convinced you to jump into the lake when it was five degrees out." The room vibrates with laughter as we think back on that time. Jejune and I continue to pass the time by thinking of old memories we share. School, Amella training, sleepovers, the good and the bad. After the emotional toll my mind and body have been through, it is nice to take time to smile and laugh. Our recounting of times is paused as Aster opens the door.

"It's been close to forty minutes," Aster says. "You guys sound like you're having fun in here."

"Mostly me," Jejune confesses. "I've been having fun laughing at her hair."

"No need to laugh," Aster says, guiding the back of my head into the sink. "She's going to be a sight to see after I wash the dye out."

I close my eyes as Aster drizzles the hot water over my scalp. I can feel the dye slide off what is left of my hair and I can tell she is almost done; the big reveal is approaching. I sense my anxiety rising. Aster turns off the faucet, dries my head with a towel, and I open my eyes to see Aster and Jejune in complete awe of me.

"Wow man," Jejune proclaims with a smile. "You… you…" Jejune is at a loss for words.

"Definitely going to have to fix those deep brown eyebrows, but other than that, you look incredible," Aster exclaims.

I turn around in my chair and finally see myself, but it is not myself, I look like a completely different person. I don't even recognize myself. I look from side to side, trying to see every angle of my new hair. From far away, I would probably look bald since the tiny hairs are extremely bleached blonde. I run my hands through my hair, the prickliness stinging my fingers.

"Rose you look badass. Even more badass than me and I don't even know how that's possible," Jejune states.

"I agree," Aster says. "You can really pull it off." I move my head back and forth in silence, taking in the new me. I do look good, but it is still so weird. "We have an early day tomorrow so don't stare at yourself for too long," Aster states, giving me a firm rub of my fresh new hair and walking out.

"She's right, got to go check on Stevey." Jejune starts to follow as I continue to gaze at myself. "I'll leave you two alone," she jokes, quietly shutting the door behind her.

I look to the ground and see my old brown hair thrown about. I take one last look at myself. I guess I do look badass as Jejune said. My blonde buzzed cut hair, my now five sphere face. I'm not Rose Pharl the six with short brown hair who works in the Film Industry. I'm not that girl anymore. I don't think I ever will be again.

After greeting everyone in the morning and going over the plan, we decided to head out right away. While Stevey plays with the other boys, Jejune is taking care of repacking all our bags. Meanwhile, Aster is tending to transform me into her doppelganger, continuing to pile makeup on my face and work her magic.

"Oh man, this is really freaky," a nervous laugh escaping her mouth as she changes my face. "You're like the twin I never had."

"Speaking of that, can I ask you something?" Aster nods as I think of the best way to ask this. The old Rose would not dare say, let alone think about this question, but it is something I have thought about and need an answer. "How come –"

"Look up," Aster says. "I got to cover your other spheres." I look up, involuntarily blinking from the dabbing of makeup. I continue on with my question.

"How come all you guys look the same?"

"What do you mean?"

"You guys, the actresses, if that's your title," I swallow, maybe I shouldn't have brought this up. "The announcement actresses, actresses on stage, actresses in all the States. You all have the blue dress, red hair, six spheres."

"Hmm," Aster simply replies. "Look back down." I revert my head back to normal, watching Aster drag more makeup.

"I'm wondering if there's a reason you all look the same?"

"I don't know," she frowns. "That's just how Veil wants us to look." Veil. Where have I heard that name before? I rack my brain until it hits me: Counting Day. That drunk blonde lady at Chard and I's table mentioned that name. "And done!" Aster shouts, lifting her brush off my face like the buzzer on a game show went off stopping the clock. Aster's shoulders bounce as she starts to chuckle. "This is really creepy."

I turn my head to face the wall that is one long mirror. A small gasp escapes my mouth as I look at this new face painted on mine. More shocking is that she covered my other spheres so now I only have one, just like her. I never thought I would have just one sphere on my face. Aster places her head on top of my shoulder and copies my star struck face. It is truly an odd site, we are not the same person, but our faces are almost identical.

"You're gonna freak out the little ones with this get up," Sid scorns, walking into the room. He jumps in the air and collapses into a pile of clothes and blankets.

"Oh my!" Jejune exclaims, also coming into the room. "Who is who," she jokes.

"Aren't you guys supposed to be leaving," Sid sighs. "Like now."

"Yes, Jean is getting the spheres to put on Rose's face and then we will all be out of your way, and you'll never have to see them again," Aster snickers at Sid. "Sound good."

"Ecstatic," he sarcastically replies.

Jean walks in with what look to be small circular white stickers. She hands them to Aster as she tells me to face her again.

"Make sure the makeup crew do not wipe off your makeup. Make sure they only take off these spheres," she says, showing me the tiny sticker in her hand. "If they wipe away your makeup it will not only show your real spheres, but your freckles will be wiped off and they'll know something is up." I nod as she carefully places the fake spheres under my eyes.

"How did you get your hands on these gems," Jejune asks, referring to the fake spheres, walking in front to watch Aster put them on my face. "People would kill to get their hands on these."

"Wardrobe crew. I get so many every month. They keep a log to make sure I'm only using them for filming. Besides, I couldn't use these to gain points on Counting Day because they wipe everyone's face."

"Damn, they've really thought of everything," Jejune says shaking her head. "Smart bastards."

"How do they feel?" Aster asks as she applies the final sphere.

"They feel fine, a little sticky." I stretch my face and wiggle my nose to get used to the feeling. "It feels weird to have fake spheres covering my real spheres."

"The stickiness will subside, but my work here is done." Aster rallies up all her supplies and I take one last look in the mirror. With six spheres added back to my face, I feel more like myself, minus the freckles and blonde hair. "Sid, tell everyone we're heading out," Aster states, leaving the room. Groaning, Sid hoists himself up to get everyone. I stand up and look to Jejune, who is staring at me.

"I don't know, it's just," Jejune shrugs her shoulders and looks for the words. "It's just freaky."

"I guess but," I stop and look in the mirror. I smile as my blonde hair shines. "I kind of like it."

"I'm sorry," Jejune leans forward with wide eyes. "Did those words *actually* come out of Rose Pharl's mouth?" Jejune shakes her head and exhales. "You know, I think this whole experience has really changed you for the better."

Before I can comment, everyone piles into the room. Violet kindly asks if she can give us a hug goodbye. Johnny and Watson shyly wave, followed by Lawrence as he stands by Pearl, still uncomfortable with her surroundings.

"Alright little man, it's time to go," Jejune says to Stevey across the room. Stevey and Charlie run with laughter towards the rest of the group.

"I don't want to go," Stevey sighs. "Charlie is my best friend."

"I know baby," Jejune says rubbing his head. "Just because you won't see Charlie all the time doesn't mean he still can't be your best friend." Stevey nods and turns to Charlie.

"I'm gonna miss you Charlie."

"I'm gonna miss you Stevey," Charlie says back. They both give each other a great big hug.

"Best friends?" Stevey asks.

"Best friends," Charlie replies.

Although we were only here for a short while, they really bonded with each other. After saying our farewells, we grab our things as Jean and Sid walk us out. As we walk down the hallway, I think back to how this all started with Jejune pointing a gun at Jean. Who would have thought everyone would be so welcoming and warm.

"Shield your eyes," Sid warns as he gets ready to open the door. Like fire from a dragon, the sun's rays breathe on us. Squinty eyed, we wait until Sid tells us the coast is clear. With the okay, we make our way up the last few steps and back into the wild woods.

"You will all definitely be missed," Jean says. "You were a nice addition to this odd family we've created." She embraces all of us as we exchange our thanks. "We will all be thinking of you and wishing for the best."

"I guess you guys were pretty cool," Sid says rolling his eyes. Jean looks at him disgusted. With his face turning as red as his fiery hair, he clears his throat. "If everything works out okay, come back and visit. I'll be worried about you guys," he quietly mumbles. Stevey runs to Sid and wraps his arms around his waist.

"We'll miss you," he says, squeezing tight. Sid looks down and wraps his arms around Stevey as well.

"What do you know he has a heart," Jejune says.

"Shut up," Sid sneers, snapping his head up at her. Stevey lets go and returns to Jejune's side, reaching for her hand to hold.

"Are you sure you don't need any help," Jean pleads to Aster.

"No we'll be fine," she replies. Jean extends her arms and gives Aster a long embrace, as if this is the last time she will get to hold her again. "We got to go now, I'll see you tonight."

With Aster leading the way, we follow suit. After a few paces, we turn back to give Jean and Sid one last wave before they go back down the stairs and remain hidden from the rest of the world. As we walk, I take in the early morning scenery. The trees cast shadows over our bodies as the sun flashes through the branches.

"JJ what do you think will be at this new place?" Stevey excitedly asks.

"I don't know little man. What do you want there to be?"

"Kids my age. Like Charlie!" he squeals. "So we can play and have fun. Do you think there will be kids like me?"

"Maybe, we'll find out when we get there," she replies, squeezing his hand. After walking some more, Aster informs us that this is where we have to part ways.

"Rose you're going to continue straight. In about two minutes you'll see the film set. When you get there, look for the chair near the mirror, that's wardrobe. That's where you'll change into your outfit, put your wig on, and get any finishing touches. All you have to do is stand on your mark and read the lines, they'll be projected on the camera. Just make sure to smile and read slow. Even if you think you're reading the lines too slow, that's a good thing. Most importantly, don't let the others get to you." Aster pauses, a hint of sadness in her eyes. "Most actresses are ones and twos, like myself. We don't get a lot of respect because we aren't fives like you guys," she weakly gestures towards Jejune and I. "So if they do make a comment, just try to ignore it." I nod, taking in everything she has told me.

"While you're filming," she continues, "we'll head to the next film set. By the time the driver drops you off we should already be there. Oh, also, don't talk to the driver under any circumstances." A confused look comes across my face as to why. "It's too hard to explain, but trust me, don't talk to the driver," she says, responding to my facial expression. "Once we meet at the second film site, we'll switch places and then you three will be on your way."

"Well," I scoff. "When you say it like that it sounds so easy."

"Hopefully it is." Aster steps forward to give me a hug. I hug her back, still surprised by the number of hugs I have received in the past twenty four hours. "I'm sure you three want some time to say your goodbyes, so I'll let you be." Aster gives us our space and begins putting on her own makeup as she walks away.

"Rose I don't want you to go," Stevey says, colliding into my thighs.

"Stevey," I say, holding his shoulders as I crouch to his level. I look into his concerned eyes framed by his crooked glasses. "You know how when you go to school and you don't see JJ for a little bit?" Stevey nods. "It's just like that." He nods again and lunges into me for one last hug. I give him a quick pat on the back and then stand to say goodbye to Jejune.

"Listen," Jejune says, adjusting her hat. "I still don't really know how you feel about the whole thing but I mean look at you," Jejune waves her hand up and down and smiles. "I've *never* seen you this confident in your life! But," Jejune swallows, the bloodshot in her eye glistening. "Please be safe. I'm going to be worried about you. I know I'll see you on the other side, but please be safe." Just as Stevey did to me, I lunge forward and squeeze Jejune who squeezes back. My quivering breath presses against her shoulder as the tension in our bodies emerge. Although Jejune is tough on the outside, I know she is just as scared as me.

"You know what the sad thing is," Jejune says, still hugging me. "I won't get the chance to see you acting on the big screen." My shoulders shake as I laugh and we release from our embrace. "I would love to get a copy of you all dressed up making the announcement."

"I'll let you know how it goes," I chuckle.

"Hey actress you're gonna be late!" Aster yells, pursing her now ruby lips. Not wanting to drag it out anymore, I continue on towards the set. I turn back and watch as Jejune and Stevey head to Aster. I keep turning back to see them until the trees consume their appearance, officially leaving me alone. The rhythm of my heart-beat matches the crunching of the leaves beneath my feet. This is it, this is *really* happening. We are really going through with this absurd plan to disguise myself as Aster. I replay Aster's tips over and over in my mind.

Smile and read slow.

The sound of my steps is replaced with voices and metal clashing, which I can only guess is the set being built. The voices get louder as I zigzag through some more trees and the film set is revealed. The set is an exact replica of the North set I work on, but it is definitely different walking onto set as the talent and not a sound person. The mass amounts of people running back and forth is slightly overwhelming as I search for the wardrobe area. Just like on the North set, the wardrobe girls are together and gossiping, looking over the top and unnecessary.

I approach their huddle as they look me up and down and then disperse all annoyed, as if I am an inconvenience to them. I politely smile, but do not get one in return as I place my bag down and hop up on the chair. An unhealthily skinny girl grabs a brush and slaps it against some makeup. Despite being petite, her hair is far from that. To be honest, I am not sure how the weight of her hair is not breaking her neck. Her purple lipstick matches the lavender glitter surrounding her eyes. Every time she blinks the shimmering reflection blinds me. Not to mention the crystals scattered throughout her hair clumping together like an anthill at her curly ponytail.

"You must be," she pauses and turns around to look through a row of hung up headshots. From the row I see Aster's face, along with other actresses. All have one or two spheres in their photos, and all the actresses are emitting the same emotion: sadness. "Aster, right?" She looks back at me, disgust painting her over the top face. I shyly nod, embarrassed to be associated with those pitiful headshots hanging for all to see. "So like I was saying," she says to the girl next to her. "She told me that she was all out of crystals."

"Oh *did* she now," the girl next to her preparing my wig replies, looking just as over the top as the makeup girl.

"Oh yeah and I told her, Karen I *know* you got those crystals and you know how I know."

"How honey," she dramatically pleads.

"I said I *know* Karen because you got the crystals in your own hair."

"Shut up! She did not!"

"Oh yes she did," the makeup girl squeals. "If Karen thinks she is gonna fool me she got another thing coming. 'Cause Karen, I ain't no fool."

"Tell her girl," she replies, snapping her fingers.

While this whole conversation is transpiring, the girl continues to apply my makeup. Both of them act as if I am not here; just another set piece. My anxiety about people recognizing I am not Aster subsides. Is this really what Aster has to deal with?

"I'm doing your lipstick so don't move," the girl says to me. Uncomfortable, I search for anything to look at as she carefully draws my bright red lips. She finishes and moves over for the other girl to apply my wig. As she secures my wig and makes the proper adjustments, the two continue with their rambling. I thought I was exhausted from waking up early, but these two are exhausting just listening to them.

"Look up," the skinny girl says to me. Without warning me, she starts to bring something to my eye and instinctively I flinch away. The girl leans back offended. "What is this your first day? Look up so I can put your contacts in."

Trying to act normal, I do as I am told. My eyelids flutter as the sliminess from the contacts seep into my eyeballs. After both are in, I squeeze my eyes and blink a few times, trying to make my eyes adjust to the feeling.

"You're all set. Your dress and shoes are behind the curtain," she gestures, waving her hand towards me. Before I can even get off the chair, the two go right back to facing one another and gossiping. Now I can see why Aster told me not to talk to anyone. If I were to open my mouth and interrupt, they would be hysterical.

As told, I sneak around to the make shift dressing room to change. With the gossipers and loud noises of the set surrounding me, it is somewhat nice to be alone in this tiny space. We have not even started filming and I am overwhelmed.

Exhaling, I grab the dress hanging up with the matching heels underneath. I begin to undress when I feel eyes watching me. I timidly look over my shoulder and notice some guys checking me out. Embarrassed, I run to the curtain and close it as much as I possibly can. Pushing those creeps aside, I slip the dress up and over my hips and slide into the heels. Ready to go, I look back at the mirror for the final product. I am mortified.

I know that the person I am looking at in the mirror is me but it is not me, I do not recognize myself. I suddenly think back to the ballroom on Counting Day, watching the actress get shot and die in front of my eyes. That is the person I see in the mirror. The same frightened baby blue eyes staring back at me. That feeling I got before I had my breakdown yesterday returns. My face is hot, there is tension in between my eyes; I hate this. I want to tear this dress and wig off me, but I have to stop myself. I have to remember why I am here.

You can do this. You have to do this.

Recollecting myself, I step out of the dressing room back into the chaos.

"Jeez what were you making the dress in there, what took you so long," the girl who put my wig on says. "Come here and let me fix your wig."

"One minute! One minute!" a production crew member yells out.

"That's the best it's gonna look," she replies.

I remain still, unsure what I am supposed to do now. I think back to when I saw Aster on set who showed up when they said –

"Where's the talent!" a man screams.

As per Aster's instructions, I walk in front of the camera and find my mark. It is easy to find the red x against the stark white backdrop. With all the lights and eyes watching me, I am beyond nervous. When I saw Aster walk to her mark, she was so confident, but I do not feel anywhere near that. I feel so small on this huge film set.

"Cueing prompter," a man surrounded by computers says.

I can feel sweat bubbling underneath my wig as the bright lights shine on me. My heartbeat is pounding in my ears and I fear others can hear it. The black lens of the camera is replaced with my lines to read.

"Camera is locked," another voice says.

Like a hummingbird's wings, my eyes dart around to take in the final moments of chaos.

"Quiet on the set," the director says, sitting behind the camera.

Silence.

Complete silence washes over the set as all eyes stare at me.

The director shoots his hand up, spreading all his fingers counting down for everyone to see and hear.

"Five."

I don't know if I am ready for this.

"Four."

What am I doing here?

"Three."

What if I mess up?

"Two."

What if they know I am not Aster?

The director mouths the word one.

Smile and read slow.

The red light glows on the camera. I smile and begin reading the lines.

"Hello, Westerners. Amella would like to wish a Happy Counting to you all. Tomorrow marks our thirty sixth hundredth and one Counting here in the States and my how far –"

"Cut!"

My smile fades and I look to the director. *Oh my goodness. Oh my goodness. What did I do?*

"I know it's early sugar cake, but could you have an *ounce* of excitement in that voice of yours," the director asks. I nod, my nerves swelling all inside my body.

"Cueing the lines from the top," the man surrounded by computers says.

"Quiet on the set," the director repeats.

Smile and read slow. Be happy, be happy, just be happy.

He raises his hand but in a fist. Waiting a moment, he points to me and the red light turns back on.

"Hello, Westerners. Amella would like to wish a Happy Counting to you all. Tomorrow marks our thirty sixth hundredth and one Counting here in the States and my how far we have come. Three hundred years ago humans were weak, frail, and delicate. Weeping in public, mourning the death of others, crying from –"

"Cut!"

Crap, I thought I was doing well.

"What are you doing with your hands!" the direct yells. Unaware I was doing anything with them, I look down to see my fingers interlocked. Was I rubbing them? Was I picking at my nails? I really don't know what I was doing. "Stop with your hands," he snaps. "Keep them by your side and just read the lines like you're supposed to. Like you always do, it's not that difficult." Annoyed, the director slams his elbow on the armrest of his chair and massages his forehead. "From the top please!"

I look to the wardrobe girls, whispering to one another looking at me. I look to the sound people rolling their eyes. I look to the man behind the computers huffing and puffing. My bones become tense and heat swims throughout my entire body. Trying to not make it obvious that I am extremely uncomfortable, I calmly place my hands by my side and stare into the camera lens, awaiting for the lines to start from the top. I take a deep breath and try to calm my mind, and the red light turns on without the director's signal. Panicked, I fumble to say the first line.

"Hell–ell–hello –"

"CUT!" the director screams. I jump back from his outburst, the muscles in my back and shoulders continue to strain. I try to remain calm but it is extremely difficult, I have never been so stressed out in my entire life. The director gets out of his chair and starts pacing as everyone watches him, awaiting what to do next.

"Is this the best that we can get?" the director shouts looking to everyone on set. "Is this the best that we can get?" he asks again. All I want to do is run as far away from this mess I made as possible. "Here's what we are gonna do," he exhales, looking at the watch on his wrist. "Everyone take a one minute recess and by everyone I mean you," he commands, pointing directly at me. "You have one minute to go back in the dressing room, figure out whatever it is you need to figure out, so I can get my footage. If you come back out of that dressing room and you can't do that, you are fired. Got it?" I am frozen with fear, anxiety, embarrassment, and shock as the entire set stares at me. Unable to speak, I simply nod. The director extends his arm behind him and points at the dressing room. "You have one minute."

Shamefully, I walk to the dressing room, my high heels and scattered mumbles the only sounds to hear. I fumble to grab the dressing room curtain as the girl who did my makeup tells me I am pathetic. I finally get the curtain to budge and close it behind me, pressing my back up against it as I swallow a chunk of vomit trying to fall out of my mouth. Not only have I ruined this plan, but I have also put Aster's reputation on the line. The director can't fire me because he would really be firing Aster. I make my way to the mirror and collapse against it, sliding down to the ground like ice gliding down a glass.

I want to go home. I want to be back in the North with my mom and my dad. I want them to give me a hug. Jejune said that this experience made me change for the better, but I do not see how because I am still not as strong as her. I may be a five but I do not feel like a five right now. Jejune also told me that the only thing I care more about than me, is me. Maybe she is right, but that is not how I want to be anymore. They are disgusted by my presence yet they do not even know I am a top sphere holder just like them. They are disgusted because they think I am a one, and I am reassuring all of them out there how a one would act: weak, frail, insecure. There are other people being affected by my actions right now. Innocent people, the ones, the twos, the threes; undeserving of consequences divulged from me. I cannot let that happen because I know Aster, who is a one, and she is far from those qualities.

Stumbling, I stand up and turn to face the mirror. I shimmy my dress down, fix my wig, and take a good look at myself.

"This is not about you," I tell myself. "This is not about getting the perfect shot. This is about showing them that no matter how many spheres you have, you can be strong." I finish my speech and, standing taller, I march to the curtain and fling it open to see all eyes on me.

Smile and dominate.

Glaring at the director, I strut back to my mark and take my stance in front of the camera. Everyone on set looks to the director and waits for him to say something. I know Aster told me to ignore their comments, but I will not be silenced by them. I will speak for the ones, twos, and threes. That is what Jejune would do and that is what Aster would want so I will speak for her.

"Yes," I declare with a newfound confidence. "This is the best you can get."

As my lines appear on the camera lens and the director looks dumfounded by what just happened, I continue to stand tall, hands by my side, and await the red light to signal my performance. As the camera records me, with the lights painting my body and the microphones amplifying my strong voice, I do not miss a beat. I pause at the right moments, flash a smile when needed, and figured out whatever it was I needed to figure out.

"…keep your spheres and do not shed your tears. Happy Counting Western-ers." I conclude with a forced smile.

"Cut!"

The red light vanishes and the muscles in my cheeks relax. The director stares at me as the chaos flies back into action. Crew disassembling equipment, computers dimming the lights, everyone yelling over one another. His eyes continue to track me as I walk back to the dressing room. I do not know if he is angry that I spoke up for myself or ecstatic that I gave him a stellar performance, either way, he is speechless.

No longer tense from nerves, my body is now high on adrenaline. I change into my regular clothes and emerge, the two wardrobe girls waiting for me. The one who looks like a glitter bomb exploded all over her walks to the adjacent table as I sit back in the chair. The one who did my hair slips the wig off, carelessly removes my blue contacts, and joins the other at the table. I remain seated, waiting for the glitter bomb to come back. Not getting up, they both look at me confused. I point to under my eyes wondering why they are not taking off my spheres.

"Oh, you want me to take off your spheres?" my makeup girl asks. "Well since you couldn't get your lines right the first time," she says condescendingly, "I don't have time to do that. You have to go straight to the next shoot." She rolls her eyes and gently fondles her hair, as if her little eye movements damaged her updo.

After her short outburst, I grab my bag and head off the set. Just like when I arrived, no one is acknowledging my presence as I leave. I am totally ignored, like an irrelevant molecule floating in the air. I do not even look back as I walk away; I want no memory of this set. Surrounding myself with trees again and no film equipment, I find a small black car waiting. Assuming that is the car to take me to the next shoot, I open the back door and hop in.

"You're late," the driver says to me. He is wearing sunglasses and dressed in all black. The car screeches and heads deeper into the woods as I frantically secure my seatbelt. Curious as to how he knows where he is going in the woods, I peer out the window and can faintly see a dirt road. Although the car ride does not last long, we enjoy it in complete silence. The car abruptly comes to a stop, and the driver remains motionless as I get out of the car. I shut the door and he immediately drives off, a few leaves fling in the air from the rotating tires.

Feeling stranded, I look around to see any sight of Jejune, Stevey, or Aster. Amongst the greenery, I spot a black hat peeking out from a log with "JJ" written on it. I walk towards the log to let them know I am here. As I start to walk, my bag is yanked backwards and I go with it as a hand covers my mouth. Panic fills my body.

"You're coming with us," Jejune says to me in a deep voice.

"Not funny." I push my way off her. Jejune laughs, her bald head glowing in the sunlight as she grabs her hat.

"I told her not to do it but she insisted," Aster says, walking with Stevey. "So how was your first day as an actress?"

I want to grab Aster and commend her for how strong she is. For dealing with those people all the time. How they blame her for everything. How they assume the worst because she is a one. Those people do not even see her as a human; they barely even saw me as a human. We were taught that people like Aster, the ones, are weak but after what I experienced today, she is one of the strongest women I know.

"I do not know how you do it," I sincerely say.

"Trust me," Aster scoffs, raising her eyebrows. "Years of practice. I can see they didn't remove your spheres. Any reason why?" I carefully peel away my fake spheres and give them to Aster who places them under her eyes.

"Time purposes." Still tacky, I rub under my eyes and pinch away the residue.

"I still can't believe this worked," Aster squeals. "But you guys got to get out of here. If any crew from the set come out and see two of us..."

"Yeah, that would be hard to explain," I reply.

"Well, goodbye." Aster wraps her arms around me. Despite receiving hugs more than wanted lately, I hug her back. I have never felt this much love and affection from a stranger. She is filled with immense joy despite the way she is treated. After hugging me, she moves onto Jejune and Stevey and heads to the set. I want more than anything to switch spheres again and take her place.

"Aster," I say to her. She turns around waiting for me to continue. "I do not think they will be bothering you anymore." Aster tilts her head curiously but smiles.

"Good to know." She turns back around, continuing her way onto the set.

"What did you do?" Jejune asks with a questioning look. I look to Jejune, mirroring her face. Jejune raises one eyebrow and I do the same.

"What are you two doing?" Stevey asks, straining his neck to look up at us. We both start laughing and Jejune swings her arms around me.

"I was so worried about you," Jejune says. "Man, why do I care so much."

"I do not know, but we should listen to Aster, we have to go."

"Right," Jejune raises her eyebrows, letting go and crouching to the ground.

She straps her backpack in front of her chest as Stevey hops on her back. "Aster explained how to get to the edge. The only thing we need to figure out is where to go once we cross the edge of the border because after that we are on our own."

"Will it be scary?" Stevey asks, dangling his tiny hands over her shoulders.

"It will only be scary if we don't make it before dark." With that, we start our way back through the woods and towards the edge.

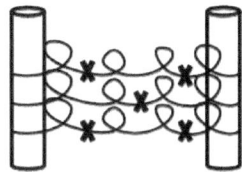

After walking for close to an hour and no sight of anyone, we take a break to eat some food to regain our strength. I tell Jejune and Stevey about acting and how I told that director off. I had to convince Jejune that I was telling the truth and that I actually stood up and said something to a superior. With our stomachs full, we continue our journey. Stevey tells us stories about school and Jejune quizzes him on spelling as I listen quietly. As our feet trail on and our mouths keep moving, we slow down our pace as we come across something odd in front of us.

Approaching closer, we notice a bright, solid thick red line painted over the ground jumping out at us from the sun's reflection. Following that line are stacked rows of barbed wire reaching just below our knees. With our shoes at the edge of the line, we look right and left and notice it stretches on and on, weaving in and out of trees and over piles of leaves.

"Is this it?" I ask.

"No this can't be," Jejune replies perplexed.

"Well what else is it?"

"No, wait," Jejune laughs. "You're telling me that with all the vein scanners, crew members, and surveillance Amella has this," she gestures to the tiny fence. "*This* is the *edge* of the West? This is the *edge* that is supposed to *stop* people from leaving?"

"Well if not that then what else?" I question.

"Why is it so shiny?" Stevey asks, reaching towards the fence.

"Don't!" Jejune cries, snatching his hand from the sharp wires. "That stuff

189

will hurt you baby." Looking right, then left, and behind us, Jejune makes sure no one is around. "Let's find out," she says.

She lifts her leg up and places her foot down over the fence. Careful not to hit the barbed wire, she watches as she lifts the other leg over. With two feet officially over the fence, she turns to face Stevey and I.

"Um," she proclaims with a smile. "That was too easy." The quiet air is quickly broken with a loud blaring siren and we all clamp our hands over our ears. "Shit, run!" Jejune yells over the thundery blast.

Panicked, I hop over the fence as Jejune reaches for a frightened Stevey screaming for the noise to stop. Without any plan or idea where we are, we just run. Run like we have never run before.

As we run, once again, my mind runs at equal speed. My parents. Chard. Frank. Fred. Jean, Aster, and all the kids they took under their wing. Are they worried? I want to tell them all I am okay. I want to let my mom and dad know that I am safe and to not freak out when I am not home at curfew tonight. That I am fine and I will be back soon I promise. Maybe come back with some answers. Maybe come back with this so called truth that Jejune so badly wants. The constant thud of my heart beating in my ears overlaps with the blaring siren surrounding us. My mind goes on racing. What about those crew members we killed. Will someone find them? Will Amella know it was us and come looking? Maybe we will find this place, but even if we do, will people believe us? Will they think we are crazy? What if there is no place and we are running in the woods to find nothing?

Suddenly the woods vanish behind us as the ground unexpectedly dips without any warning, flinging all our bodies forward. Not being able to stop our motion, we begin rolling like rag dolls over and over until our bodies come to an abrupt halt, finally colliding with dry, flat land. Trying to catch my breath, I weakly look up as dust and pebbles press against my face. This dry, flat ground stretches on for miles before rising to form red stained, jagged mountains; it is breathtakingly beautiful. In the middle of this vast land are small tents and massive rectangular cars with tables and chairs outside each one and there are people. Wait. There are people! Is this the place? Did we really find it or am I hallucinating?

Before I crawl my way to Stevey and Jejune who are struggling from the fall, someone approaches us. She is walking calmly, almost floating towards us as her thick layered clothes blow in the wind. Her tangerine, wavy hair is draped in front of her reaching her hipbones. Her skin is pale like white cream and honey, her eyes sunken in and wide like a wolf. Although wide, her eyes are mysterious and bold with black heavy makeup smeared over and under her eyes, covering any spheres she may have. Her raised cheekbones isolate her slim lips as magnetic orange and subtle yellow flowers form a circle around her head as long, beaded necklaces create a carnival of colors throughout. She stops about ten feet away from us and slowly extends her arms out next to her. She holds this stance for some time, looking to us as we remain in pain sprawled out on the ground, desperate for air in our lungs. A comforting smile forms across her face as she tries to reach her arms out even further.

She takes a long deep breath in, shakily closing her eyes and tilting her head to the sky. With the sun shining down, the black under her eyes transfix me.

"Welcome," she softly says. "Welcome to Cali."

END OF BOOK ONE

Acknowledgements

I would first like to thank the brave men and women who serve and have served our country in the United States Armed Forces. You have sacrificed your time and lives in order to protect all of us. Without you, I would not have been able to write this book.

As mentioned in my dedication, thank you to my family. You have and will always continue to support and love me. A special thank you to my Yia Yia for always telling me I would be a star. To my extended family who I love as my own: Niki, BAE, GiGi, Jewel, Diane, and Shaney Boy.

To my amazing husband, thank you so much for all your support every day and believing in everything I do. This short blurb is not nearly enough to express my gratitude for you. I love you now and forever.

To all my students. Thank you for making me a better teacher every day and showing me that you are never too old to learn something new.

Finally, to you, the reader. Thank you for diving into the world of Amella and joining Rose, Jejune, and Stevey on their adventure. I hope you enjoyed.

About the Author

V. Angelo is an American author. Graduating with a BA in Psychology and a Master's in Education, Angelo used her studies as inspiration in writing *Spheres* to take a deeper look at how we perceive ourselves, perceive others, and perceive the world. When not writing, Angelo can be found dancing, reading, and binge watching reality television. Angelo's world revolves around educating, inspiring, and sharing her love for imagination, and she hopes to show this through her storytelling. *Spheres* is Angelo's first novel. Visit Angelo's website and follow on social media to stay up to date on future publications, news, and upcoming events.

Website: www.vangeloauthor.com

Social media: @vangeloauthor

www.ingramcontent.com/pod-product-compliance
Lightning Source LLC
Chambersburg PA
CBHW050842180626
46814CB00007B/2584